INSANITY

By

Rusty Hodgdon

Where does the violet tint end and the orange tint begin? Distinctly we see the difference of the colors, but where exactly does the one first blending enter into the other? So with sanity and insanity.

Herman Melville (1819 - 1891)

This book is a work of fiction. Names, characters, places and incidents are products of the author's over-active imagination or are used fictitiously. Any resemblance to actual events or locales or persons, living or dead, is entirely coincidental.

KEY WEST, FL

OTHER NOVELS BY RUSTY HODGDON

~SUICIDE

A new arrival to Key West, Dana Hunter only wanted to be left alone to write and enjoy life after raising children and a divorce. But a brief argument in a bar, and the later witnessing of a suicide, lower him into the hellish depths of facing murder charges and police corruption from which only a good lawyer and the love of a woman can resurrect him.

~THE SUBWAY KILLER

Anthony Johnson is a handsome, charismatic pimp who is suspected of murdering several college co-eds. When Mark Bowden, a young, impressionable Public Defender is assigned to represent him, he quickly finds himself cajoled by the beautiful women of Johnson's stable into going far beyond the bounds of ethical legal conduct.

COMING:

~THE EYE

Prologue

The Town of Cary, California lies in the crook of the elbow formed by the intersection of Interstate Routes 205 and 5 in the Central Valley of the San Francisco Bay Area. It is physically separated from the City by the Bay by a broad swathe of hard scrabble ground that runs north and south on its western border. But it is also worlds away from the sophistication and beauty of that City. With a population of around fifty-five thousand people, it ranks in the bottom tenth percentile of average annual income and high school graduations in the State. It is mostly rural, but a large industrial area bounds the northern and eastern perimeters of the town.

It was there, in that area five years ago in 2003, that a fire erupted in the lot at Harry's Tire Emporium. When the firefighters first arrived, they discovered an enormous, and highly illegal, flaming pile of tires covering almost seventy acres. No one knew how long it had been there, because there were no records of its existence.

It soon became apparent that it would be impossible to contain the conflagration. The toxic smoke kept the firefighters at an ineffectual distance, and none of their extinguishing agents, especially water, had any impact on the oozing inferno.

They had to let it burn out, over two years, casting a pall of black soot and smoke over Cary the whole time. When the last flames flickered and went out, they discovered that the site had also been used as an industrial dump, with metal, rotting barrels and containers scattered about the lot.

✟✟✟
Chapter 1

The gray-green liquid oozed slowly at first. Starting as a mere gelatinous glob near an outlet valve on the huge, cast iron tank which lay on its side amidst the spotty grass and hardened mounds of rubber and rubble, the glob grew, steadily, forming a stalactite, reaching, almost finger like, for the ground. After several months, a puddle formed, and finding only loose dirt, the insipid substance seeped further downward, creeping, crawling into the earth, forming tentacle branches, gallon after gallon, until the tank emptied.

The rains came, saturating the earth with the mixture, joining it with silent, underground rivulets, carrying it inexorably to the water table and into the wells and faucets of the town of Cary, California. Etched into the hard metal of the tank were the words "Superior Chemical Company: N-dimethyltryptamine" and "Danger – Do Not Touch". The tank lay, neglected, in the abandoned, yet still smoking, yard of the Tire Emporium.

✝✝✝
Chapter 2

She etched the line above her eye slowly with her finger, seeing the movement backward in the mirror. Janna had not noticed this one before. Usually, she was pleased with the reflection. Twenty-eight years was just not that old. Her dark, almost black hair was thick and curly. People generally told her she was cute, with a pleasant, round face and small upturned nose. Oh, she knew she had gained some weight, but no one could say she was obese – only pleasantly plump.

But over the past several weeks something peculiar had been happening. It seemed that her normal, tiny wrinkles – for instance, her previously barely discernible crow's feet – had become more visible, even protruding. Why even the pores on her nose appeared gigantic, seeming craters. She also had noticed an unusual flush in her pale complexion.

Was she getting ill again? She was taking her medications. Religiously. The thought that she might again be engulfed in that Hell terrified her.

Well, no time to dwell on negatives, she thought. We are all things to Christ Jesus. And she always had the delight of her life, five year old Britney. Since Britney had come into her world, except for a brief spate of postpartum depression, she had been mostly symptom free. Only occasional disconnected voices, or sudden, but short-lived moments of panic. And when Britney's father disappeared from the scene over a year ago, the major source of stress in her life was gone.

Yet the bad thoughts had been intruding into her consciousness lately. Hannah, the "perfect child", and the child of her best friend, Elaine, had been teasing Britney incessantly. Didn't they both realize just how sensitive Britney was? It infuriated her that Elaine wouldn't be more proactive and discipline her daughter.

Her father's light knock at the door to the bathroom, and gentle admonition that the service was to begin in fifteen minutes, interrupted her thoughts. It was a real problem to have your Pastor as your father, not to mention to live in the rectory immediately adjacent to the church. The church building was small, only seating about a hundred parishioners, and the rectory was even smaller: a squat, two story structure housing only two bedrooms and a bath and a half. It was situated right on the cusp of the residential part of town and the vast fields of corn, rice and alfalfa to the east. The industrial area lay only a mere mile away to the north.

She could never escape, never be occasionally free –

maybe even wild. Oh, she loved the Lord, she knew. She enjoyed singing in the choir, leading a young woman's Bible study. But increasingly she was considering the impossible, that maybe the Bible was not infallible. Like, what was? If only she could do something really crazy. Just once.

╬╬╬
Chapter 3

Dr. Bradford Wilson had wanted to be an Ob/Gyn since he was a little boy. His best friend's father was one. He owned a large gentleman's farm, where they played endlessly in the hay loft of the barn and rode horses all day. Brad, having come from more modest means, dreamed of the day he would have the excess income to enjoy such luxuries. He also loved telling his parent's friends at their numerous dinner parties what he wanted to be. Always got a good laugh, especially, although more discreetly, from the ladies. He also enjoyed the little tingling in his groin area, even at age six, when he thought about it.

Medical school did its best to wring any emotions or feelings out of the process. There was even a time when he didn't think about it. But his fascination with the female anatomy – the sense of mystery, even a little repugnance – always won out.

He first joined a physicians' group in Cary. Yet he found that his practice, possibly because of his cinematographic good looks and 6' 1" stature, soon outpaced that of the others. It only took three years before he bought his own building and opened shop for himself.

It was shortly after he moved in – maybe it was the sense of empowerment he gained from establishing his own business, in his own office – that his obsession began to take hold. Each time he was with a patient, even during routine exams, he could feel the stirrings that ultimately grew into a full-blown hard on. Yet, so far, he had never acted out on his tumescence.

‡ ‡ ‡
Chapter 4

Martha couldn't take much more. Billy was getting increasingly out of control. Her worthless husband George was no help. She didn't know how to handle a fourteen year old. He had been foisted on her by that pitiful sister of hers, Grace, who had no grace, or much of anything else for that matter. She was probably in some drunk tank at the moment. Grace had stayed in touch for a couple of months after depositing Billy on her doorstep three years ago. But it had been over a year now of absolute silence.

It wasn't bad at first. Billy was well-behaved, seemingly happy to be in a more stable environment. Yes, the space was cramped in the tiny, two bedroom bungalow, but the money from the state for his support helped out.

Billy was now a tall, gangly adolescent. His hormones were raging. Why just three weeks ago she had caught him with that little tramp from down the street. What was her name? That's right. Maria. The little whore Maria. They were lying down on the couch together when she came through the door after grocery shopping. She knew they were in there and surprised them.

Ever since she had locked Billy in his room at night — the only one occupying the second floor attic space. She left a basin so he could pee. Made him come directly home after school and get right to his studies. The weekends were getting tougher. Harder to keep track of him. She was thinking he should be confined to his room during the day as well. You just can't trust young teenagers these days. Next thing you knew he'd be getting some girl pregnant and then her problems would really start. No. That wasn't going to happen to Martha. Not on her watch. No way.

‡ ‡ ‡
Chapter 5

Dr. Richard Henderson sat in his cramped office in the Science Department building at Hart University, tackling another PHD dissertation. It was the part of the job he liked the least – a job that he had hated for years. The dissertations had become increasingly esoteric, and in Dr. Henderson's view, worthless over the fifteen years he had been reviewing them. His was usually the lone dissenting voice in the approval of the candidate's work; he had rejected the vast majority of them.

His passion was research, especially conducting studies. They allowed him to travel, take needed time away from the school and the bothersome students, and could be very lucrative. In ways the university would never imagine.

The Doctor's musings were interrupted by a gentle knock on the door. I don't need any visitors at this time of day, he thought to himself. Probably some grad student trying to browbeat me into a higher grade or influence me into approving his doctoral thesis.

Dr. Henderson yelled toward the door, asking the interrupter to enter. Two of them came into the room. The first was a man in his late fifties, heavyset, with a large mustache that slightly curled at the end. The other was definitely younger, say about thirty – tall, physically fit, with clear, intelligent eyes.

The older man spoke first: "Dr. Henderson, I presume. I'm Henry Sampson, Deputy Director of the Saint Claire County Board of Health, and this is Sam Pritchard, my assistant. Sorry to barge in on you like this, but we've been trying to reach you for several days. Didn't you get our messages?"

Richard knew he was terrible at returning phone calls, especially when he didn't know what the caller wanted, and even more so when he had, as in this case, an uneasy feeling about the purpose of the call.

"My apologies. As you can see," and with this he swept his arm across the room with its stacks of books, loose papers, and other paraphernalia of academia, "I've been extremely busy. So what can I do for you?"

Sampson continued to be the lead man. "We are investigating the spillage of some chemicals in Saint Claire County, near the towns of Cary and Oxford. It occurred at the old Tire Emporium lot where they had the fire. It came from a tank from the now-abandoned chemical plant – Superior Chemical, to be precise. It took us quite a while, but we understand the particular chemical at issue was one you had them synthesize. I was told you performed some studies with it. So we just want to talk to you about it. Find out what kind of studies and whether or not there may be any danger to the good people of the County. That's our job – to find these things out."

Richard paused for a moment. He knew damn well what chemical they were talking about. Superior had only made one for him. He couldn't believe, after all these years, he was being brought back to that particular study. Or that the chemical had been stored, rather than destroyed, as he had insisted to the president of the company. He spoke carefully.

"I don't specifically recall that company, or the chemical. The location doesn't ring a bell, either. Why do you think I was involved in its production?"

Now Pritchard cut in. He was not as folksy or friendly as his boss. "We know what chemical it was. Its name was conveniently etched on the side of the holding tank. It was N-dimethyltryptamine. Commonly known as DMT. Moreover, we obtained all of the company's records on this particular substance, and the only end user of it was this University. Further investigation revealed you used it in a certain project about ten years ago. That's why we're here."

Obviously they did their research well, Henderson ruminated. I should have guessed they wouldn't be here unless they had.

"Well, if it is DMT – and I don't believe it yet, because I was assured it would be properly disposed of – you have nothing to worry about, because it is highly unlikely the chemical could remain in its active, and potent state, after this passage of time."

Pritchard spoke again: "Actually, there seems to be some difference of opinion on that point. Before we came, we asked the scientist who consults for our local board – Timothy Lynch – do you know of him? He got a second opinion from another respected guy. A Dr. Wilfort. I forget his first name. They both think that, given the right circumstances, the chemical still might pose a hazard. We want to know from you exactly what dangers may be lurking out there. You're supposed to be the expert on this."

"As I already said, I don't perceive any danger. The molecules of DMT simply could not have withstood the elements for this long. But even if they did, it could not have been distributed to a large number of people. There's simply no system that could spread it. Do you have any indication that it has affected anyone in the county?"

Sam Pritchard looked hard at the Doctor. "No empirical evidence. But we're receiving some anecdotal reports that are a bit disturbing."

"Please don't bother me with anecdotes. I'm a scientist, you know. We don't operate on that basis."

"Nor do we," Sam interrupted, to Dr. Henderson's great irritation. It showed on his face, but Sam ignored it, and continued:

"You asked if we had any indication the DMT had any impact. We've gotten calls from two respected psychiatrists in our area. They say they've noticed a worsening in the condition of their more seriously ill patients. One even relayed to us that he's taken on three new patients in the past two months. He hasn't had that many in years. Two of these patients exhibited schizoid ideation."

"There's more," Henry added. "We receive quarterly reports from all physicians, hospitals, healthcare providers of any ilk. The incidence of reports of emotional disturbances is way up. We can't say at this stage the leakage of the DMT is responsible. But it's enough to cause some alarm."

Dr. Henderson didn't like what he was hearing. He had privately thought for several years that he should have personally overseen the destruction of the chemical. But he wasn't going to admit that now. He needed an exit strategy.

"Gentlemen. I appreciate your visit but I have a class I have to teach, so if you'll kindly excuse me."

"We understand, Doctor, and we appreciate your time. I hope you don't mind if we follow up with you later if the need arises," Henry responded.

"Of course. Contact me any time," Henderson said as he escorted the men to the door.

Chapter 6

Janna exited the bathroom and rapped loudly on Britney's door on her way down the hallway. "C'mon honey. Got to be at church in ten minutes. Let's not be late like last time." No response from the other side of the door.

Janna had to stop, turn around, and go back. Now she was aggravated. "Britney, get your fucking ass out that door, NOW!"

Did those words come out of her mouth? She had never spoken to her daughter, much less any one else, in that way.

Britney appeared at her door with a look of shock on her face. She had her mother's thick dark hair, and plump little body. She couldn't speak, and tears formed in her eyes. This was enough to get Janna crying.

"Honey. I'm so sorry. I can't believe I said that. Please forgive me. You will forgive me, won't you?"

Janna reached down and took her daughter in her arms and hugged her close.

"Mommy promises never to use such horrible words again. Never!"

Britney squeezed her Mom tight and said: "Mommy, I forgive you. I'm ready for church now. Let's go."

As they walked hand in hand downstairs, Janna remembered how, lately, the horrible words had been increasingly intruding into her consciousness. Fuck. Cunt. Cock. Words she would never think of, much less speak, until recently. What was the matter with her? Was the Devil taking over her soul? She decided she was going to devote her Sunday school class to the devil within us.

╬ ╬ ╬
Chapter 7

Pastor Dan Gleason was just finishing a final review of his sermon for that Sunday when Janna and Britney entered the kitchen.

"There are my two beautiful girls. On time, too. Miracles never cease." Dan always spoke in a large, booming voice, as if he were perpetually giving a sermon. His chiseled good looks and silver mane made an observer overlook his seventy plus years. Britney ran up and gave him a hug.

"Good morning Poppi. Can we get some ice cream after church today? We haven't done that in a long time. Please!"

"Honey. Maybe next week. I've got a deacon's meeting right after the service. Kind of an emergency meeting that was just called."

"Daddy. Is something the matter?" Janna had not heard of an emergency deacon's meeting in almost a year, since that adulteress had been banned from the church.

"Nothing major, sweetheart. Nothing for you to worry your pretty little head about. We just found out one of our members – can't mention any names right now – has a personal website containing some inappropriate material. We have to decide what to do about it."

Janna was immediately titillated. What kind of material? She wanted to check it out right away, but knew better than to press her father on the issue at this time. She'd learn soon enough. The church was a gristmill of gossip, rumor and innuendo.

✠ ✠ ✠
Chapter 8

Dr. Bradford Wilson knew he was in deep shit. It was the second notice, this one by certified mail, from the state Medical Board. He hadn't even opened the first one. He knew what it was about. A husband of one of his patients had called him three weeks ago, threatening to come over and pound the crap out of him. Brad was sure one of them had filed a complaint.

He had managed to control himself for a while after starting his practice. Until just about a year ago. He didn't even remember the patient's name now. She had come in with a very bad yeast infection. Nothing unusual. Yet Brad was immediately smitten. It was not her visage, or very large breasts. It was more her skin: the color of light walnut, and as smooth and unblemished as a baby's rump. And long, long legs. Endless legs.

When she confessed she was very nervous about an internal examination, he suggested sevoflurane, a potent combination of nitrous oxide, commonly known as laughing gas, and oxygen, and she accepted. Then his urges took on a life of their own. He had always been able to control them.

Not this time. While she was under, he first performed cunnilingus on her, and then pulled up her johnny and masturbated on her stomach. It was not until her eyes fluttered and began to open that he noticed a white, crusty deposit in her belly button. His clean up had been too hasty. He did not know to this day if she discovered it and suspected anything.

The floodgates were now open. His next opportunity came about a month later. This time it was a girl in her late teens, who again evidenced fastidiousness about the process.

He was bolder. Using Astro Slide, a quick drying lubricant, he entered her gently, so as not to cause any subsequent pain or irritation. He pulled out at the last minute, and again his orgasm drenched her stomach. He was more careful about wiping up this time.

The most recent episode – the one that led to the phone call, and probably the certified mailing – was his most reckless. Again, another particularly gorgeous patient. After delivering the drug, for the first time he had a hard time getting an erection. So he sat in a chair and began masturbating, fully intending to rape her. Suddenly a young girl, a part-time receptionist he had just hired, burst through the door. He had forgotten to hit the lock. She let out such a scream that the patient came partially to. The girl turned, ran from the office, went home and never came back to work. Brad had to quickly put it back in and zip up his pants. At the time, he was sure the patient saw something. Now he knew she had.

He had to be more careful. The urges were taking over.

Chapter 9

Brad's thoughts were interrupted by the irritating voice of his wife, Mary.

"What is that that came in by certified mail? Didn't you get something a couple of weeks ago too?"

"It's nothing. I just forget to get my annual registration in on time. I'll take care of it at the office today."

Mary accepted the explanation without a passing thought. "Please don't forget to take the trash out today. You forgot yesterday."

"I won't. Did you pick up my laundry?"

"Yes, dear. It's hanging right in the downstairs closet."

She couldn't even bring it upstairs and hang it in mine, Brad thought. He was getting particularly aggravated by her lack of energy and effort these days. Hell, she stayed home all day. The girls were in school. How much was there to do?

Mary had her own thoughts. Our conversation never extends beyond the mundane any more. We only talk about what it takes to do the most basic of tasks. When's the last time we actually sat down and discussed a *personal* issue? Years, she bet. But maybe that was because their lives had become so ordinary. Her husband had not demonstrated a desire for sex in over a year. And the prior time had probably been six months before that.

She knew, at age thirty-five, she was still very attractive. The mirror could not lie to that degree, even accepting the subjectivity of the viewer. She also sensed it from the furtive, and not so furtive, looks she got from guys. It had taken a lot of effort to keep so trim, and thankfully she had the luxury of a daily visit to the gym. It was only her husband who seemed to have no interest. Her day ahead loomed as all the others did – a contrived series of events simply to kill time – grocery shopping, getting her nails done, taking the girls to get some new shoes. She had to break out of this rut.

Chapter 10

Billy was late again from school. This was going to be the last time that happened. Martha jumped into her car and went looking. She knew where to go. The kids loved to hang out by the basketball courts off of Elm Street. She would sometimes drive by the spot just to see if she could catch some of them kissing or fondling each other. Public displays of affection. How she hated that.

Sure enough, as she approached the courts, there was Billy, holding hands with that whore, Maria! Martha pulled over to the curb and yelled out the window: "Billy! Get your butt over here this instant!"

She saw the crimson pallor spread quickly over Bill's countenance. She enjoyed his humiliation. Billy quickly dropped Maria's hand and turned toward her. "Aw, c'mon Mom. I'm just playin' some B-ball. Let me go." She had lately insisted he start calling her mom, or mother, or some variation of it.

"I mean now! Not a minute from now. Not two minutes. NOW!" Martha screeched.

Billy reluctantly walked to the vehicle and got in. "Ma. I

wasn't doin' anything. Just wanted to have some fun. I was heading home just before you came."

"I told you last week that you were to come directly home after school. And this is how I get repaid for taking you in? Feeding you. Maybe you shouldn't be allowed to go to school. I'll home school you. That's what I'll do. It's the only way you'll get a proper education." Actually the thought had just popped into her mind. It was perfect. She could keep an eye on him twenty-four/seven.

"No Mom. I need to be around people my own age some of the day. I'll do better. I promise I won't stop anywhere on my way home. I'll come right home. I promise." Billy was pleading now.

"Shut up!" Martha screamed. "My mind's made up. I'll order some of those home schoolin' materials. Keep you home 'til they come in. You can read and study some of your regular work until then."

Martha felt grand. She had found serendipitously a remedy to her dilemma. She needn't worry about George. He'd do what she told him.

⊹⊹⊹
Chapter 11

Billy was beside himself. He was trying to be good. His grades were still excellent. He just didn't think stopping briefly at the courts was a cardinal sin.

It was hard enough the way his mother had treated him. What a relief when she dropped him off with his aunt! Yet he was not too young to fail to notice a gradual change in Martha's treatment of him. She had never been affectionate. Not once had she hugged or kissed him. He didn't expect that. But in the beginning there had at least been a reluctant acceptance of him. Now she seemed to be irritated by everything he did.

Billy decided to talk to George about it. George was always very quiet and reserved. Billy had never once seen him stand up to his wife in any matter. But maybe that reserve masked a wisdom that Billy could tap into to help him through the present situation.

Billy approached George when Martha was busy in the kitchen preparing supper. As usual, George was in his Easy-Boy, half reading the paper, half watching the news on the small TV situated in the corner of the den.

"George, can I talk to you about something?"

George took at least a half minute to slowly set the paper down and look at Billy. He was not happy about the interruption.

"What's on your mind, boy? Can't you see I'm busy?"

"Well, I promise to take just a minute of your time. And can we agree that anything we discuss now will be just between us guys?"

There was a momentary look of panic on George's face, which quickly changed to anger.

"Don't ever try that on me again. I tell Martha everything. If you've got something to say, say it, or say it in front of her."

"Well, I mean, it's not all that important. It's just that . . . that I think Auntie has been very rough on me lately. She always seems to be angry at me. Now she doesn't want me to go to school. She wants to home school me. I won't get to see any of my friends. I like school. I even like most of my teachers. Could you talk to her about it? Please!"

George abruptly got out of the chair, the paper falling in a cluster at his feet. His lips were trembling. "Don't you ever ask me to question Martha's judgment again. She always knows what's best. Always!"

He walked into the kitchen and Billy could hear an animated discussion in the kitchen. Suddenly Martha emerged with a carving fork in her hands. She was livid. She brandished the weapon at Billy, screaming at him. "Get up to your room right now! There'll be no dinner for you. Get up there!"

Billy forlornly and fearfully climbed the stairs and entered his bedroom. He heard the door slam behind him, and the outside lock click shut.

╬╬╬
Chapter 12

Sam Pritchard returned home that night certain that Henderson was being less than straight with them. Not that Henry would know. In Sam's brief tenure with the board, Henry had not issued a single violation notice, much less sought court action against offending parties. He loved to pontificate about his duty to the public, but his actions revealed a different side: don't ruffle feathers, coddle the wealthy, and life will go smoothly. Sam took this work much more seriously. He had not suffered through the Masters, and then Doctorate program at Southern Cal in Public Health to be a yes man to polluting corporations.

"Hi baby!" He yelled as he walked in the door. "I'm hoooome!" As corny as he could say it.

Miranda and he loved to portray the Nelson family, or any other conventional TV family, as often as they could. "In the kitchen, Ozzie dear," came the reply from within.

Miranda and he had been married three years. No children yet, but they certainly planned on it. Mandy, as he usually called her, had to first finish her last year at Stanford law. She was brilliant, cute as a button; and the total love of his life. All more corny expressions, Sam thought as he hurried into the kitchen for the next best part of his day: getting a huge hug and salacious kiss from the sexiest woman in the world.

After they locked in a tender embrace, and more than several deep kisses, the hackneyed banter continued:

"What's for din-din, June?"

"Just the usual, Ward. Meat loaf, mashed potatoes, and green beans."

"Oh not again," Sam protested in mock horror.

Sam stayed in the kitchen while Miranda finished preparing the shrimp scampi and blue cheese wedge salad. He poured two glasses of sauvignon blanc.

They talked easily about their respective days, leaving out, for this time, anything serious. Sam only touched upon his brief meeting with Henderson; Miranda recounted an argument she got into with her torts professor during class.

Only Mandy could best a professor in a public forum, and still get an "A" at the end, Sam thought. Her combination of intellectual tenacity and old school charm was irresistible, to any male, at least.

At dinner, over candlelight and a well-set table, as was their usual wont – they were both in agreement it was the little details that made life enjoyable – they let the conversation wander to more taboo subjects. They spoke as would best friends.

Miranda was having difficulty with her moot court partner; the guy just wouldn't cooperate and let her write most of the brief. He should have recognized by now who was the better legal writer, she joked. The problem was, it was true, Sam observed. One of her professors, after obtaining her permission of course, had personally copied one of her exam answers and distributed it to his next year's class, proclaiming it the best he had seen, and a near perfect response to the question.

Sam elaborated further on the Henderson meeting. The increasing evidence of peculiar behavior among the people of Cary had already been a frequent source of discussion between them.

"I had the distinct feeling that he just wasn't being truthful with us. Henry, as usual, was clueless. He claimed it was impossible for the stuff to have survived this long, and also denied it could be spread through the water table. He wouldn't even acknowledge the possibility of such a scenario. That's directly at odds with what I gleaned from our guys. Remember Tim thought there was a chance, albeit remote, of the DMT remaining potent and capable of distribution, even after this passage of time."

"It's understandable there might be a difference of opinion on those issues," Mandy countered. "Why don't you get Tim to do some more research for you? That's part of his job."

"Yeah, if I can get Henry to authorize the extra expenditure," Sam groaned.

"We're friendly enough with Tim and Sally to ask for a favor, if necessary. Remember I helped them with their dispute with their neighbor over the driveway encroachment. I think he'd do it for free. Assuming that it comes out that it's possible the DMT could be in our water supply, you could confront Henderson with the information and see if you can get him to help you understand the ramifications on the community."

"That's a great idea, Mandy. I'll call him first thing in the morning."

It was time to go to bed – another highlight and the best part of the day in the Pritchard household. They did not let the fire go out in their home.

Chapter 13

The next morning Sam gave Tim a call. As the phone rang, he realized he had not been a good friend lately. It was tough maintaining social contact. Never seemed to be enough hours in the day. But he knew that was just a lame excuse. It was mote that, after making and fielding twenty to thirty calls a day at the office, he had little motivation to make social calls. Another lame excuse. I'm going to get better, he promised himself. Heck, it it wasn't for Mandy, they probably wouldn't have any friends.

Tim was not in at first, but called back within a few minutes.

"Hey Sam. What's up? How's Mandy?"

"Not much Tim. She's doin' great. How 'bout you and Lori? Heard you guys just came back from vacation. How was it?"

"Fantastic. Did the Napa Valley again. Our third time around. I could go there every month. Wait. I could live there!"

"Yeah, and I'd have to come by every month and scrape you off the floor. I know you and Lori get sideways every time you go," Sam said half-jokingly.

"Aw. It isn't *that* bad. We enjoy the scenery too, ya know."

"It is beautiful. And there's nothing the matter with letting go every once in a while. Mandy and I have only been there once, and I can barely remember a minute of it."

They bantered back and forth a while longer, Sam remembering how much he enjoyed Tim's company. But it was time to get to the point.

"Tim. Henry and I met with that Henderson guy the other day. You remember, about that DMT leak we discussed. I didn't feel he was forthcoming. I appreciate the research you did before. But Henderson gave us no real answers. I thought he'd clear everything up. Give us a straightforward explanation of the potential dangers. All he could do was keep repeating that it was impossible for the stuff to be affecting anyone, but he had to go real quick when we tried to pin him down on the scientific basis for his opinion."

"Yeah. That sounds like the Dr. Henderson I've heard about. Arrogant as hell," Tim cut in.

"Well, here's my dilemma. I know if I go to Henry at this point for funds to pay you to continue your research, he'll say no. There's just not enough yet to get him to authorize it. I know him. Do you think you could look into it a bit more – on the QT – so I'd have a more solid basis to press him to go further with this? You don't have to go overboard. I'd deem it a personal favor."

Tim only hesitated for a few seconds. "Of course I'd do that for you Sam. You want more info on the chemical properties of DMT, and the probabilities on whether or not it could get into the groundwater, and how long it could stay there. Right?"

"Yeah. Scientifically. Something with some real punch to it. That will get Henry to look deeper into this problem."

"I'll get it for you. I don't know where I'll come out on it, but I'll find an answer. I also think, Sam, while I'm doing this, you should go back to Henderson and find out more about the nature of his study. What were his goals and techniques. What angle did he have on it. I think I mentioned to you before, the little I did look into the effects of DMT on humans, the more scared I got. It's really weird stuff. A guy studied it about ten years before Henderson. Wrote a book on it. Concluded it got to people in a whole bunch of different ways. It all depended on their individual personalities, and their environment when the tests were administered. It was a drug that maintained the subjects in a dangerous state between dreams and wakefulness. Often they couldn't tell the difference. Some of the dreams weren't so nice. There was a suggestion that some of the subjects – those with preexisting mental conditions – never got beyond that state s. I sure hope that crap isn't in our drinking water."

"Tim, I can't thank you enough. I hear what you say. The little I know about it, I hope to hell it isn't in our water too."

╬╬╬
Chapter 14

The young women looked earnestly at Janna as she entered the room. Janna wore the expression of a woman on a mission. She had something important to teach these girls today.

"God bless you," Janna said as she sat down. "Please open your Bibles to 1Peter 5:8 and 9. Sara, could you read that passage for us?" Sara, a slim girl of sixteen, hesitated, not anxious to be the focus of attention in the class. She read, haltingly:

Be self-controlled and alert. Your enemy the devil prowls around like a roaring lion looking for someone to devour. Resist him, standing firm in the faith, because you know that your brothers throughout the world are undergoing the same kind of sufferings.

"I've been giving a lot of thought to the devil lately," Janna said. "How we all have to be constantly on guard against his schemes. He wants to take us over for his own whenever he can. What are the other names for the devil?" she asked the class.

No one answered at first. "Satan," yelled out two of the students in unison.

Then Sally, one of the brightest among the young people gathered that day, intoned quietly: "Beelzebub." There was a murmur of disquietude in the class when that word was mentioned.

"Yes, you're right. Satan and Beelzebub," Janna responded. "Does any one know what Beelzebub means?"

Sally spoke up again. "Lord of the Flies."

"Very good, Sally." Janna continued: "How many here have read the book or seen the movie 'Lord of the Flies?'"

A few hands went up. Janelle's was one.

Janna spoke to her: "Janelle, can you tell us what it was about?"

"Well, I don't remember exactly, but I think a bunch of school kids get stranded on a remote island when their plane crashes, and then they start fighting with each other."

"Yes, that's a good summary, but do you know why they started fighting?"

Sally spoke up this time: "Because they were all boys!" A few of the girls sniggered.

"But do you think it would have been that much different if it had been all girls? I don't think so. I think what the author was trying to say is that, left to our own devices, without the authority and discipline of the Lord, we will allow

Satan to take over our lives, and do things we would never otherwise have done. Unimaginable things. That's why it's titled 'Lord of the Flies.' Beelzebub took over those children and made them his own. Beelzebub is the prince of demons."

‡ ‡ ‡
Chapter 15

The pastor hated Deacons' meetings. Although he was
the titular chairperson, these headstrong men often ran the
meeting the way they wanted to. Dan knew his ultimate place.
He was the spiritual head of the church, but the congregation,
including these Deacons, paid his salary and benefits. How
would anyone else deal with two hundred and fifty or so
bosses, he ruminated. It was even harder after Helen had died.
She was his confidante and sounding board. Just talking to her
about the pressures in his ministry helped him.

Sometimes these meetings would go on for hours. The
subject matter being addressed tonight was also distasteful.
Ernie Bates had been a congregate of the church for over
twenty years. A stalwart: a good family man, had run the youth
program for several years. This thing about the website was
very disturbing. Dan hoped they wouldn't have to discipline
the man, much less report him to the authorities.

When he walked into the church conference room, he
could sense the seriousness of the matter. The normal banter
that preceded the meetings was noticeably absent. Dan said
hello to everyone, and opened the gathering with a standard

prayer asking for wisdom and grace from God. Then he sat down to discuss the matter.

Unfortunately, Bob Anders spoke up first. 'Unfortunately' because Bob was a very large black man who had a serious prior criminal record. Yes, he had served his time in prison, found the Lord, and was actively involved in the church. But everyone, in Dan's view, and he emphasized everyone, was deathly afraid of him. Bob was intimidating both because of his size and the roughness jail had instilled in him. He usually got his way, even though that way had led at times to disaster.

For example, there was the time Bob had taken in a young man who had been recently paroled after serving three to five for grand auto theft. Bob was instrumental in convincing the Board to hire the kid as an assistant custodian. One morning the staff came in to find the church van and all of the silver - the offering plates, Communion chalice, and candelabra - long gone. Never did find the guy, or get the stuff back. Bob simply shrugged his huge shoulders and said it was the work of the Lord. No one disagreed.

"Who called this meeting?" Bob began. Without waiting for an answer, and none was immediately forthcoming, Mr. Anders continued: "I know Ernie well. He's a friend of mine. He's told me he's bullshit that we're gathering here to discuss him without him being present. So I invited him. He's right outside to answer any accusations you might throw at him. But I want you all to know a false accusation thrown at Ernie is one thrown at me as well. Understand what I mean?"

Everyone in the room nodded that they understood. Ernie came into the room. A deacon named Hal had brought a laptop into the room. He went immediately to Ernie's website: "The Bates Family." Hal became the *de facto* MC of the proceedings at that point.

"Is this all about my personal blog?" Ernie asked. "It's just pictures of my family and friends. Get-togethers, vacations, holidays. Also some things that struck me as funny. What's wrong with that?"

"Let's just take a look at the whole thing," Hal replied. "It'll speak for itself."

Hal hit some keys, and the home page came into view. "As you can see, the current material is innocuous," Hal said as he scrolled through. "Just photos of Ernie's two daughters, Veronica and Tamara. Here's Veronica at her piano recital; Tamara's fourteenth birthday party. Ernie added all this yesterday. To get archived material you have to scroll all the way through and then click on 'earlier posts'." Hal did just that

— went to the end of several pages and clicked the left mouse button on the portal to prior material.

"Again, we have family events: Mildred's sewing class — she brings in some good money with that, doesn't she Ernie?" Hal interjected while turning in Ernie's direction. "Now we have shots of some friends over for a barbeque - many of you will recognize the Shaw's, Billy and Barbara, and Kate and Steve Olson. But look here, if you click on this photograph of meat on the grill, you find an embedded side-site. You wouldn't know it was there unless you just happened on it."

Hal clicked, and a profiled image of a cute, young girl with golden blond curls appeared. She was just about to eat a foot long hot dog that had been doctored to look like a penis. The caption under the image read: "Super Seven Incher - It'll blow your mind!"

"Somebody put that in there!" Ernie rose as he screamed. "I've never seen that before! They're out to get me!"

"Sit down, Ernie. I'm sure there's an explanation for this," Dan said calmingly. "Let's look at the entire thing, and then you can have your say."

Hal went to an earlier blog. "You'll recognize pictures of Ernie's boat; the family dog, Bosco. A cute Dachshund. But again, it you double-click on Bosco's photo, here's what you get."

The front cover of a book was displayed. The title was: "How To Live With A Huge Penis: Advice, Meditations, And Wisdom For Men Who Have Too Much." The author was Ernie Bates, and superimposed over the caption was a fuzzy photograph of a very large penis.

Bates was beside himself. He got up to leave but was restrained by Bob Anders, who growled, "Ernie. Looks to me like you got some explainin' to do. Sit your ass down." Ernie sat down.

"There's more," Hal added. "I found this video hidden in the photo display of the Cary Town Choir. It's entitled: 'Satan In High Heels'. Let me play it for you."

A human body, apparently that of a woman, was dancing provocatively in black high heels, a G-string, and bare breasts. The identity of the person was obscured behind a rather elaborate mask, clearly of the Devil, replete with curled horns and flaring nostrils. The room looked eerily like Ernie's finished basement, but cleared of all furniture, pictures, anything that would offer a more precise clue as to its location and ownership. The woman danced elaborately to the Rolling Stones "Sympathy For The Devil" building to a crescendo which ended in her fucking herself madly with one of the horns, which she had ripped off during the dance.

Everyone in the room sat dumbfounded. Embarrassed. Incapable of speaking,. Ernie had his head in his arms, sobbing.

Dan relieved the tension by suggesting Ernie go home so they could discuss the matter. Ernie gladly took the suggestion, leaving without a further word or looking back.

‡‡‡
Chapter 16

The doctor's thoughts strayed to his boring schedule for the day as he drove into work. The same endless cycle of looking at a woman's genitals. Oh sure, there would be the occasional interesting case. Like the woman who had masturbated so hard with a dildo she called the "Rabbit" that she tore the membrane of her vagina. It took him twenty minutes to finally elicit from her what had happened. He had her bring it in for her follow-up exam. He was fascinated by its motion – the different settings which caused the base, and then the head to gyrate at increasing speeds. He almost asked her to leave it with him.

But that was the exception. The vast majority were routine and resulted in no more than a prescription for chlamydia or a yeast infection. His mind happily roamed to what might be. He never knew when that ideal specimen might walk through his doors. But he knew it when she did. He might not choose one for weeks. Let a few possibles enter and exit. Can't get greedy. It made his days, even weeks, bearable; holding off, waiting. Maybe today, he imagined. It had to be just the right combination. The right looks, the right body, the right circumstances. One who wanted a general anesthesia; one in which he could find an easy excuse to ask his nurse assistant to leave the room for several minutes. It had to be just right. Maybe today.

╫ ╫ ╫
Chapter 17

The address was not easy to find. Frankly, it was in a pretty run-down part of town, Mary thought. She wasn't happy about that. She had been thinking for quite some time of trying this out, but now she wasn't quite so sure. Was it something a physician's wife should be doing? Of course, she said to herself. Some of her girlfriends had tried it; it was good exercise, and also a little sexy.

The sign came upon her unexpectedly: "Bob's Dance Studio." It was set in a block of low, nondescript brick buildings that ran along old Highway 44. Across the street was a scrap metal dealer. She pulled in front of the building – there weren't many cars parked on the street – and fidgeted in the vehicle for a few minutes before finally summoning the courage to go in.

Carrying her small duffel bag with a change of clothing, she entered into a small vestibule with two cramped offices to either side. Bells jingled as the door opened. Only an old, beat-up desk, two chairs and lamp graced their interiors. Seeing a plaque that said "Studio",and a doorway directly ahead, she went toward it, only to be met by another woman exiting. The woman was definitely younger, very pretty, petite, with a dancer's body. They exchanged a cursory "Hi", and Mary passed into the room.

It was large, mirrored on all four walls, with an aging but well-polished hard wood floor. Four metal poles were set into the floor and ceiling at each corner. Several padded folding chairs and a couple of couches were arranged around the perimeter. She was surprised to find no one else around.

A door suddenly opened from one side, exposing a changing room, and a man who appeared to be in his early thirties came out. He was dark, about six feet tall, with thick, long black hair pulled back into a ponytail. He also had a dancer's body: slender but very muscular, a small butt, and long legs. He wore a tight, black T-shirt that flattened against his developed pecs and biceps, and well-fitted nylon sweat pants.

"Mary, is it?" He said as he approached her with a smile, revealing polished straight white teeth, his hand extended.

"Yes. And you must be Bob." He was very good-looking, she said to herself. In a rough, sexy sort of way.

"You're here for the pole dancing lesson, aren't you?" His black eyes pierced hers as he spoke. Mary nodded in the affirmative.

"Looks like you might be the only one. Two other gals just canceled. But if you don't have any prior experience, it will be good to have a one-on-one. Is that okay by you?"

Mary was a little unsure about that. She didn't know this guy at all. Plus she had never touched a pole while dancing, much less slithered around one, and she didn't want to humiliate herself. But, hey, just being here was a step out of her mundane existence. What difference did it make if she got a little personal attention?

"Okay by me," she said with the sweetest smile she could muster. "But I'm a neophyte, so you've got to be patient with me." By his expression of confusion, she realized she was going to have to tone down her vocabulary a bit. "You know, I'm new at this," she added.

"That's fine. There has to be a first time for everyone, right? And anyway, you've certainly got the body for it." His eyes ran down her shapely frame as he said this. Usually this visual undressing might have made her feel ill at ease, but from him it was slightly titillating.

"Why don't you change in there," he added, pointing to the door from which he had just exited. "I'll be right out here."

Mary went into the room, and put on the clothes she had brought. She was glad she had not been too conservative, and had brought her favorite, tight fitting short shorts and a tiny halter top that exposed a good portion of her round, perky breasts. Strangely, she would have been a little embarrassed had there been any ladies at the lesson. But in front of Bob, she felt it was appropriate.

When she came out, electronic music was pumping out of speakers hidden somewhere – in the ceiling? – and Bob was stretching.

"Let's get warmed up. It's very important. We don't want any injuries," he said, still smiling.

Mary stood next to him and began to follow his lead, looking primarily at the mirror ahead. First slow toe-touchers: with feet together, then spread further and further apart. Bob next moved into several graceful maneuvers he described as his own personal blend of Tao Chi and dancing exercises. Mary was pleased that she was able to follow him without much effort. She also marveled at his balance, his steadiness juxtaposed with his strength. After a few minutes, Bob asked her to come over to the nearest pole.

"We're going to start with some basic moves which I'd like you to practice first. Then I'm going to show you some advanced moves just so you can see what you want to work toward. Get some resin on your hands first."

They both went over to a dispenser on the wall. "Just a light coat at first. You can increase the amount if it's not enough, but less is better." Mary complied, putting only a dusting on her palms and fingers.

Bob walked over to the adjacent pole, dimming the lights as he did so. At the same time, he hit a switch, and a light show of purples, roses, and azure blues erupted around the room, strobing to the music.

"I would like you to follow my moves as best you can. Don't worry about anything except starting to feel comfortable with the pole. We're going to begin with the basic fireman move. You've seen firemen going down a pole before. Just pretend that's what you're doing, and be sure to grip the pole with your knees and the soles of your feet."

Bob took a short leap, and deftly grabbed high on the pole as he had asked Mary to do. He held that pose. Mary did the same, and thought, I've done this plenty of times as a kid. This is easy.

"Now, slowly start to climb the pole, again using your knees and feet to grasp, and then slowly lower yourself back down. As you're doing this, be conscious of the music. Let your movements flow with the music."

Mary followed Bob's movements up and down the pole.

She was already starting to feel comfortable, and definitely enjoyed watching Bob. His skin rippled as his muscles worked. It reminded her of nature films she had seen of a cheetah tensing to take flight after its prey.

"Okay, that's very good, Mary. You're a natural at this. Really. I can tell."

Mary couldn't suppress her glee at hearing this, and gave him her best smile.

"Now, let's do the same thing, but this time I want you to cross your feet around the pole, so that your clamping action is more with your lower calves. It's a little bit harder, but I know you can do it. Climb up and down again, but on the way down this time, let's try a brief spin. Only 180 degrees though. Hang on tight."

Mary started in the position she had already learned, then slowly crossed her feet and let go with her knees and let her feet take over. This movement pushed her crotch lightly against the pole. The sensation was not at all unpleasant. As she went up and down the pole, the feeling became increasingly erotic.

On the third trip down, she let her body spin , with control, until her feet touched the floor. Then back up again, allowing the pole to slide between her legs, gyrating slightly to the pulsating music. She spun with more abandon on each subsequent climb, feeling a freedom of motion and exhilaration of spirit like never before. Sweat beaded at her brow and flowed from her body, causing her nylon top to cling tightly to her skin. She was in her own world now, a world of free flight, of sensual stimulation.

Bob's gentle hands on her shoulder barely interrupted her reverie. "Mary, don't overdo it now. You look so gorgeous on that pole. I'll say it again: I've never seen someone take so easily to this dance." He lifted her gently and effortlessly as she released her grasp. He smelled vaguely of musk and mint, a nice combination.

"Why don't you sit down and rest for a bit, while I show you some more advanced moves … just so you can see what you're getting yourself into."

With that he leaped, cat-like, gracefully, to the upper part of the pole, and spun quickly down, revolving six times before touching down lightly with a full leg split. Then another spring upward, but this time he suddenly inverted, hooked his feet around the pole, and spread his arms out. Pulled himself up, began rotating faster and faster, and extended his entire body straight out, perpendicular to the pole. Brought his feet back to the pole, then his entire body, again horizontally, but holding with one hand, seemingly suspended in air, as if he were flying next to the pole. As he dismounted, he did one twist in the air, and landed at her feet with hardly a sound.

"I performed several moves in quick succession. The first was a jump and slide; then a carousel. Next an inverted crucifix; the flag; and ending with the superman. There are scores of other moves. If you stick with it, I know you'll be able to accomplish all of them."

Mary was mesmerized. She had never seen such dexterity, such grace, in any dancer. It was more a delicate combination of gymnastics and dance.

Over the next half-hour, Bob helped Mary perfect the beginning moves she had started with, then gently arranged her arms and legs in different positions to show her variations on those moves: hooking her knees around the pole, pushing away from the pole with both arms, then only one. Sometimes stationery, sometimes revolving. At the end, she was exhausted, and had to steady herself against Bob's shoulder when she first stepped away.

"I'm sorry. I didn't realize I was so dizzy."

Bob put his arm around her for a few seconds. "You have nothing to apologize for. You were amazing. You have a right to be tired."

This last tactile moment between them made her realize how long it had been since she had been touched by a man – and how much she had missed it.

"Well, I'd better be going now," Mary finally said. "I think I've gone past my allotted time. It's been over an hour."

"That's no problem at all. You must come back. Because I think you have so much natural talent, I'm going to try to arrange the next few sessions between us to be private. Would that be alright with you?"

"That would be fantastic!" Mary said. And she meant it. She had not been so turned on in years. In fact, she couldn't wait to come back. She grabbed her clothes and left without changing, but not without looking back and giving Bob her sexiest grin. He would not mistake that one, she thought.

✝✝✝

Chapter 18

After locking Billy in his room, Martha went to bed to read. She wasn't all that tired. How to deal with Billy was consuming her. Was she being too harsh? No, she quickly retorted to herself. Nobody else was there to make sure he had a proper upbringing. It was all left up to her. Dear George, snoring contentedly next to her, was useless. Sometimes she actually wished he'd stand up to her, assume some authority. But he never did.

Eventually she dozed off, the bedside lamp still on, the book fallen off to the side. She was awakened, or so she thought, by a rustling sound at the foot of the bed. It was as if someone was walking by and had rubbed against the cover. She tried to open her eyes at first, but couldn't. It felt like they were stuck shut. Must have some seepage that has crusted over, she observed to herself.

Then she distinctly felt the presence of something next to her. It was the same sensation she had once experienced when she had taken a walk under some low hanging, high power lines. Her skin tingled, the hair on her arms stood up. Now, similarly, she sensed she was close to some enormous power source. Why even her thoughts seemed to be interfered with. She could not focus or connect the strings of questions rushing through her brain.

The force fields became palpable when she was lifted from the bed and carried upward. Still she could not get her eyes open, nor could she speak. Martha only knew that her body was in motion, gliding, easily, outward. It was not unpleasant – just unfamiliar. Next she was whisked through an opening of some kind, the pressure differential lightly popping her ears. Finally she was laid down on a hard, cold surface.

Then the pleasantness suddenly ended. Sharp, hot probes were being pushed into her skin: hundreds, no thousands of them. The pain forced her eyes open into slits, such that she was barely able to perceive what was going on around her. This was a minor blessing, for what little she could see terrified her. Mechanical beings of some sort, about the same size as human adults, robotic but somehow amazingly fluid, were moving around her; some applying the probes, others extracting fluids from the areas of her body around the probes. She was lying in the middle of a huge room, bigger than an airplane hanger, possibly even a stadium. Bright lights, lasers, multicolored, blinked and scanned around the interior. When she felt she could not stand the searing pain any longer, she was again lifted up and carried, for what seemed an eternity: years, decades, flashing by in minutes, time compressed into a tiny capsule.

She awoke, the sense that a lifetime had transpired still fresh in her mind. Now her eyes were open wide. She turned, expecting everything to be transformed: George older, maybe not even around any longer. But there he was, just as she had left him, talking small gibberish in his sleep as was his habit. The room had not changed a bit. The only remaining indication of her trip was the throbbing pain throughout her body. That was real. Therefore, the experience had been real, she thought.

Fearful that possibly what she observed around her was not real, she shook George hard: "George! Wake up! I need to talk to you now!"

George jumped out of his skin. "What!? What is it? What's wrong?" he yelled, assuming a defensive posture, his hands and arms in front of him to deter any attack.

"I just had a terrible dream. At least I think it was a dream. It was horrible." Martha caught herself. The experience of the dream was still so recent and clear, that she could not discern between her present, waking state, and the dream state. Wouldn't George, or anyone else, think her absolutely insane if she related what had just happened to her as true? Of course they would. "Oh never mind. I just had a nightmare. That's all. It's over now."

"Jesus, Martha. You scared the piss outta me." George was still shaking. "I thought there was somebody in the house."

"I know. I know. But don't take the Lord's name in vain. Go back to sleep."

George gladly obliged. But Martha had no chance of going back to sleep. She wondered if she could ever sleep again. There was no way she could re-live that experience.

‡‡‡

Chapter 19

At about the same time that Martha and George had retired for the night, Billy was just finalizing his plan of escape. He could not stay locked up for another night. He wouldn't use the damn bed pan again. He was trying to obey, to be good. But boy, was it hard. Aunt Martha was getting tougher and tougher. He was now locked in right after dinner, and only let out just before breakfast. One time he had to crap so bad he had to go in the pan. That was really gross.

Maria had suggested he find a way out and meet her some night. The prospect scared him silly, but also titillated him. At least the windows weren't locked from the outside. His attempts to sneak some rope from the garage into his bedroom failed when George suddenly appeared as he was lifting the coil from a hook. Luckily Billy had been able to cover his movements by pretending to be checking a light bulb directly above where the rope was hanging. He had seen enough TV, however, to try another tactic: tying together the bedsheets, covers, anything that would allow him to reach the ground from his second story jail.

Knotting the cloth was difficult; everything was so

thick. After several attempts, though, he felt that he had created a sturdy enough escape line, and was willing to test it out. Maria and he had agreed tonight would be the night.

Waiting until he was sure his aunt and uncle were fast asleep, Billy tied one end of the sheet-rope to the doorknob of his bedroom door, which he knew would not budge, and tossed the other end out the window. It came to within six feet of the ground. He was sure that he could drop that far easily; but could he jump high enough to grab and climb it on his return? He was willing to take the chance. Maria was waiting.

It was more difficult than he thought to orient himself on the window sill; to kneel, carefully turn around, and take that first leap of faith. Carefully Billy inched his way down the tied together sheets. He was at the end!

He dropped to the ground with a thud. Had Auntie and George heard him? He crouched for a minute to see if any lights went on, or someone yelled for him. Nothing. Grinning from ear to ear, Billy made his way to the prearranged meeting place: the woods behind Maria's house. They had walked through the area many times. The weather was delightfully cool, with an almost full moon giving ample light for the journey.

As he got close, he gave the signal – a high whistle that

only he had perfected. No reply. Billy suddenly wondered if all his efforts had been in vain. Maybe Maria got caught sneaking out. Or maybe she'd gotten cold feet. Then he heard it. A melodious songbird. Only Maria could mimic that one. Billy sighed in relief.

He hurried toward the sound. Maria appeared from the shadows and was in his arms in an instant. They hugged awkwardly at first, then comfortably as they settled into each other, recognized the others' touch, body. Maria smelled like fresh cut daisies. As they kissed, haltingly, Billy tasted a slight hint of mint. It was altogether delicious.

They sat down on some moss under a tree, and started their teenage banter. "Wow, wasn't that scary getting out?" "Do you think your parents heard you?" "Isn't this neat being out so late?" They also innocently discussed their day in school, that they had not been able to see each other, small talk about Maria's friends Sandy and Julie.

After an hour, as they had agreed, it was time to go. They parted reluctantly. This was puppy love at its purest. A last kiss — sweet, soft, the bare trace of a tongue.

Billy was euphoric as he approached the house … until he saw the light on in Martha and George's bedroom and in the kitchen. He was discovered, he thought in panic! The

-65-

euphoria quickly changed to absolute terror.

Billy walked around the house twice to see if there was any movement inside. No light was on in his room, anyway. He had to get back inside pronto. He went to the hanging sheet and jumped as high as he could. He was just able to grab the cloth about a foot from its end. Pulling himself up with all his might, he reached for the window sill at last. Almost there!

Just at that moment, one of the knots gave way and he fell backward in free flight the twelve feet to the ground. He could could not suppress the scream that involuntarily raged from his lungs as he traveled through the air. The impact knocked the breath out of him. Billy was sure he had broken his back, or neck, or whatever; but more than sure he had awakened the entire neighborhood.

He lay on the ground for at least a minute before he could breathe again. As he peered upward at the sky, still flat on his back, he saw his room erupt in light, and a moment later Martha's contorted face appeared at his window.

Chapter 20

Tim left a message for Sam on his home phone exactly six days after their last conversation. Said he had something important for him, and also suggested they combine the business end of things with a social visit. Why don't they and the wives meet for dinner some time?

Mandy heard the message come in. She really liked Tim and Lori. They had been out together several times in the past, and the conversation flowed easily and freely. Lori was well educated, energetic – and maybe a bit too sexy – but Mandy wasn't the jealous type. She knew she had Sam right where she needed him.

They also weren't afraid to let their hair down and speak honestly about subjects that were personal in nature. Nothing *too* personal. Just deeper than the normal verbal pablum that was dished out by most of their casual acquaintances. She called Sam at the office.

"Hi babycakes. What's doin?"

"Oh hi Honey. Nothin much. Same ole same ole. Nice hearing from you so early."

"Well, I couldn't wait any longer to hear that sexy male

voice. I'm just in my panties now, ya know. Nothin else."
Mandy hoped someone was nearby Sam when she said this.
They wouldn't be able to overhear her, but it sure made Sam
squirm. He was super in bed – very uninhibited, loving,
sensitive – but he did have a prudish streak when it came to
public discussions of sexuality. It was her favorite way to tease
him.

"Okay, okay, I've got the visual," Sam played along.
"But sorry, no one around." He knew her tricks.

"Just heard a message from Tim. He's got something
for you. But wants to discuss it over dinner amongst the four
of us. Is that alright with you, sweet buns?"

"Yeah. Sounds like fun. We haven't seen them in some
time. But I've got to warn you. The 'something' he's got for me
is additional research on the DMT. It may not be nice. I would
like your opinion on it, so it's good we'll hear it together."

"Just hope it doesn't spoil a good meal," Mandy said
disconsolately.

Chapter 21

The Pritchard's and Lynch's decided to meet at La Trattoria, a small Italian restaurant over a half-hour drive from Cary. The selection was made on the basis of the superior food, and also its distance from town where prying ears would not be present.

The couples met first at the bar for a quick, and welcome, drink, and then migrated to their table. It was obvious they genuinely liked each other. As they usually did, Sam and Mandy decided to split their meal: veal marsala and an iceberg wedge salad with blue cheese dressing. The Lynch's were not so spartan — each ordered their own meal — Tim an osso buco and Lori the chicken parmesan. The first bottle of wine, a splendid combination of Merlot and Cabernet Sauvignon, quickly disappeared, replaced by another in short order. The couples were not Bacchanalians, nor were they Puritans. They enjoyed a time out with good friends, food and wine.

They caught up on what was going on. Tim and Lori had twins, two boys, Matthew and Mark, who were constant fodder for funny stories. The parents had gone out the prior

Saturday night with some friends and left the kids with a babysitter. Tim and Lori decided to invite the friends back to their house for a nightcap. When they walked in, they found the entire living room had been turned into a tent city, with the twins sound asleep somewhere underneath. The adults had to sit at the kitchen table to have their drink.

The ladies chatted across from each other on another subject, and Tim and Sam had a chance to do some man talk.

"Sam, are you still doing your target shooting?" Tim asked.

Sam's passion since childhood had been marksmanship. His dad had bought him his first gun, a .22 caliber rifle, when he was twelve. That's just the way it was in the rural area where Sam grew up. It was a rite of passage for any young male to learn how to shoot.

Sam had taken to it like a duck to water. At age fifteen, he won the junior state championship. It continued from there, culminating in a third place finish at the nationals. Not too shabby. He had been blessed with a sharp eye and very steady hand. He needed a special cabinet to house the various trophies and plaques that evidenced his skill.

"Yeah, I still keep up with it. Go to the range at least weekly. But no more competition. Just not enough time. You know how it is."

"Yes, I certainly do,'" Tim replied. "Seems like my life now is work, the kids, keepin' the house up. But I love it. Never been happier. I love being married, havin' kids. There's never a boring moment."

"From what I hear about the twins, that must be very true."

When dessert arrived after an hour of eating, drinking, and free-flowing conversation, the talk turned to the subject at hand. Tim introduced it. He spoke primarily to the ladies first:

"Mandy and Lori, you both know that Sam and I have been discussing the recently discovered spillage of DMT from the Superior Chemical Company. The big question in our minds has been, could the chemical have gotten into our water in a strength to have any effect? Is that a fair statement of the issue, Sam?" Sam nodded in the affirmative.

"What I've found, unfortunately, is that there's no clear answer. First, DMT, in its synthesized state, is a clear liquid. The seepage from the tank was a thick, greenish sludge. It appears when DMT sits undisturbed for a long time, it's very corrosive. The Superior Chemical tank was old even before it stored the DMT. Most of what you can visibly see on the ground around the tank is actually crystallized iron."

"Do you mean plain old rust, honey?" Lori interjected.

"Not quite. It's a combination of rust and the eaten out insides of the tank. And the DMT."

Sam spoke up next: "If I remember correctly, DMT deteriorates rapidly by itself. But if it's combined with other molecules, it will attach to those molecules, and take on the life expectancy of the other substance. Is that right?"

"Exactly," Tim said. "And here, where that substance is cast iron, it could last quite a long time. Years. Even decades."

"So what you're saying here, Tim, is that it's certainly possible the DMT could be active," Mandy asked with a worried look on her face.

"Yes, Mandy. But that still doesn't mean it was able to find its way through the ground into the water table. The ground around the tank was saturated with the mixture. But so far we haven't discovered any DMT in the drinking water. That's a good sign, but it's not conclusive. The amount of synthetic DMT required to have an effect on humans is miniscule. Not only that, DMT is found naturally in some plants, and also in humans. Even if we could find it in the water, it might not have come from the spill. Testing people for it would be senseless because we would find it in them anyway."

"But how else can you explain the odd things that seem to be occurring?" Sam said. "The increase in psychiatric problems, the worsening in those who had pre-existing symptoms. It just seems too coincidental."

"I agree with you, Sam. Prior research has shown DMT has some pretty insidious influences on people. But what's happening could be just that. Pure coincidence."

"Or it could be kind of a reverse placebo effect," Mandy offered. "People begin to hear that others are exhibiting erratic behavior – and they start acting weird."

"It's not all a dark picture," Lori said with a coquettish smirk on her face. "I just read that participants in the Henderson study also felt more sexually turned on. It heightened their sensual experiences. This could be a good thing."

The foursome laughed in unison. "Leave it to Lori to elevate the discussion," Tim joked.

They ended the night with sincere good-bye's and hugs. On the way home, Mandy could tell something was bothering Sam. "Why so quiet, lover? I didn't think the report on the DMT was all that bad."

"I don't know, Baby. I was just hoping for something more definitive. I have this nagging feeling that we're just seeing the tip of the iceberg now. That the floodgates of hell are about to break open on this town."

Now Mandy was more concerned. "I hope you're not right, Honey. I just hope you're not right."

✝✝✝
Chapter 22

Janna felt a little better. Discussing how she was feeling with her Sunday School class had a cathartic effect. Still she sensed something was not quite right with her. Was there really a Devil? Did he have a bodily form? It was one thing to read about him in the Bible, in the abstract, and another to experience his spirit invading hers. She decided to take Britney shopping to take her mind off things. That's what a good shopping trip should, and could, do.

They went to the Crossroads Mall, the only one within the town limits of Cary. After eating at a fast food restaurant, and stopping at WallyWorld, they sat down on a bench in the main atrium. People watching was still one of Janna's favorite past times. She and Britney enjoyed a game where they tried to guess what each adult person did for a living, and where they might be now heading. They talked about several passers-by. Then Britney pointed out a man in black horn-rimmed glasses and a white shirt buttoned at the sleeves and collar, and proclaimed him an accountant on his way to buy some new socks. Looking around, Janna spotted a woman in a dowdy house dress, her face directed at the ground as she walked, giving her a depressed, but also furtive look.

"See that one there?" she asked Britney., while pointing at the lady. "I bet she isn't working, and just hangs around her house plotting schemes against people. She has no friends, is jealous of everyone, and wants to get back at people who enjoy themselves. Now she's going to buy some blank stationery so she can write nasty, anonymous letters to those she thinks have slighted her. She, or someone close to her, will die a horrible, painful death."

"Mom!" Britney blurted out." "That was awful. I'm sure she's not like that at all. I believe she has a mean husband who never talks to her, and she's just very sad. That's all."

This exchange seemed to take the air out of the fun of the game, so they got up to go home.

"Hey there girls. What 'cha doin'?" It was Elaine, and her daughter Hanna. Janna had not seen them in several weeks. Thank God. Hanna was cuter than a button. Her golden curls flowed down the nape of her neck, her blue eyes shining. A tough act to follow, thought Janna.

"Did ya buy anything good? Look what we got!" With that, Elaine pulled several outfits out of a bag. They were from a very expensive children's boutique down the street from the Mall.

Can't even buy from the Mall, Janna said to herself. Not good enough for you. The clothing was stunning. Nothing Janna could afford.

"They're really nice," was all Janna could mutter. But Britney held each outfit against Hanna, and excitedly talked about where she could wear them. She seemed not to have the slightest jealousy, or the slightest inkling of the rancorous bile that was rising in her mother's throat.

"You ought to come over and both of you can try them on. I'm sure they'll fit you too, Britney," Elaine said lightheartedly. "Why don't you bring Britney over later on, Janna? The girls haven't been together for a while, and we could catch up ourselves over a cup of coffee. Or maybe something a little stronger," she said with a wink.

The friendly easiness with which Elaine spoke only infuriated Janna more. How could she be this way to her face when privately, she was sure, Elaine ridiculed them? That pleasant smile definitely shielded a spiteful heart.

"We'd like to, but I promised Dad that we'd spend the afternoon with him," Janna lied. "Maybe some other time." She grabbed a reluctant Britney and walked away without further comment.

"Mommy, why can't we go?" Britney lamented. "I

haven't spent any time with Hanna in a long time. We were with Poppi all last weekend. Can't we go see them today?"

"Shut your mouth," Janna said between clenched teeth. "You don't know what you're talking about. You don't know what that woman is saying about us behind our backs. As far as I'm concerned, we'll never see them again."

Britney broke into tears. "Mommy. I just don't believe that. Hanna's my best friend. I couldn't stand it if I never saw her again. She's never said anything bad about us."

"You don't know, honey. You just don't know."

Janna knew.

✠✠✠
Chapter 23

The pastor loved the Eucharist. He wished he belonged to a denomination that celebrated it more than twice a year. Still, at least his interdenominational church believed in the doctrine of transubstantiation.

That was extremely important, for Dan had experienced a sufficient number of services to feel — no, to *know* — that the bread and wine took on the physical manifestation of Christ's body and blood. He had prepared a special sermon on the Eucharist: in fact, devoted the greater part of the past month to it. In his view his church had grown a bit stagnant. The Holy Spirit simply wasn't moving in the body of the congregation the way He should.

The Bates incident had also shaken him. The man had been a pillar of strength in the church and the community. What had gotten into his mind to put that trash on his website?

Today, Dan was going to try to change that. Move over Jonathan Edwards! This sermon was going to be one for the history books.

The final hymn had been sung, and Pastor Dan

introduced the subject matter of his sermon. He continued:

"We are about to celebrate the Holy Eucharist. We all know its source. At the Last Supper, Jesus said, 'Take this bread and eat it, for it is my body, in remembrance of me. And, take this wine and drink it, for it is my blood, in remembrance of me.' Now some would say the bread we eat and the wine we drink today are simply that, bread and wine, like you could purchase at the local convenience or grocery store. But I tell you it's different."

Several in the congregation responded with an "Amen," and there followed a slight murmuring throughout.

"For the Lord Jesus would not leave us with mere bread and wine. What kind of memory does that engender? Most of the world eats and drinks those on a regular basis. No, for the Christian, these otherwise mundane substances take on a new form, just as our Lord told us we would take on a new form when we believed in Him and were saved."

Again, a few more "Amen's" from the listeners, interspersed with a "Praise the Lord," and "Speak it Pastor."

Dan went on, raising his voice ever so slightly, his deep baritone enunciating each word with appropriate force and emphasis.

"They are no longer food and liquid; they are the actual

flesh and blood of Christ, transmuted by the Holy Spirit, so that we can feel, and taste, and smell our Lord in a way we could never otherwise do. This is the true memory of Jesus. That is what allows us to experience the Christhood the way God intended us to."

With this the church body collectively stood to its feet. Most had their eyes closed, their arms outstretched, outwardly petitioning their Lord for His forgiveness and blessings. Dan asked that the bread and wine be distributed to the congregation.

As this was happening, Dan went on: "I am convinced that the reason for the complacency, the bitterness, the infighting I see among us is a direct result of our failure to appreciate the full experience of the Eucharist. How can the Spirit move in us with all of His power if we do not have Jesus, in all His glory, inhabiting our bodies? And He can not indwell fully unless His flesh and His blood are *actually* in us. As each of you partakes of the bread and the wine, I want you to experience this reality, and to seek God's forgiveness for your transgressions."

The congregation ate and drank. At first there was silence, but then a commotion erupted in one of the back pews. A lady had fallen to the floor and was moaning. Dan saw that it was Martha, a long time member of the church. Her husband, George, looked on with consternation. Suddenly, in a front pew, two congregates simultaneously stood, fervently beseeching God to forgive them, tears running down their cheeks. More around the sanctuary either knelt or stood, literally crying out their petitions to the Lord. A few laid on the carpet and spoke in tongues. The entire church was in bedlam. Pastor Dan had never seen anything like it. This was beyond his control. He tried to restore order, shouting above the pleas and unintelligible utterances, but to no avail. He finally simply walked out of the building and went home, deeply disturbed by what he had just witnessed.

╬╬╬
Chapter 24

It was not until toward the end of the day. But almost as if on cue he entered the examination room, and saw her for the first time. Brad could not believe his eyes. She was stunningly beautiful. About twenty-five. Glowing auburn hair that seemed to reach all the way to her butt – which itself was a work of art – small, tight, sheathed in and framed by her short skirt. Hadn't he sensed this would be the day?

As with all new patients, his nurse had taken the initial information. She was in for a routine exam. It had been three years since her last. She was the nervous sort – hated the doctor's office, especially this kind. It was Brad's job to make her feel comfortable. Very comfortable.

"Hello, Miss Shaw." She was not married, he knew. "I just have a few more questions to ask you before we begin. Would you like anything to drink? Coffee? Tea? Water?"

"Some Jack Daniels straight up would be nice," she quipped.

At least she had a sense of humor, he thought. But oh, how he would have liked to throw down some Jack and coke with her.

"Well, that would be nice. Sarah and I have been talking about installing a fully stocked bar in the waiting room," he joked back, motioning toward the nurse that was there in the room with them. "Probably would increase business."

Miss Shaw giggled. "Yes, I think it would."

"Sarah, I think Miss Shaw and I are fine now," Brad said with an eye toward the door.

The nurse, with a little hesitation, excused herself. Not without a brief, and concerned glance back at the doctor. Brad didn't even notice. He was altogether absorbed by Miss Shaw.

"Now Miss Shaw," Brad began.

"You can call me Vanessa, Doctor," she interrupted. "I've never liked the 'Ms., Miss' thing. Do you?"

"No I don't." This was better than he had imagined. "If that's the case, please call me Brad. I know doctors are supposed to be higher than gods, but I've never subscribed to that opinion."

"Thank you," she said with a smile that could have conquered a continent. "I feel much more at ease already."

Brad was beside himself. He could barely keep from shaking with desire. "That's great. But I have a suggestion. I want to make sure you stay at ease. A lot of my patients like me to administer a mild sedative before the exam. It's called

Sevoflurane. It's a lot like laughing gas. You just breathe it through a mask. You won't feel, smell or taste anything. Except you will feel great. Relaxed. Happy. After about fifteen minutes, you'll be fine, and there are no after-effects. How do you feel about that, Vanessa?"

"Sounds OK to me, Brad. Anything to get high," she said with coy bemusement on her lips.

"Oh, this will get you high alright, Vanessa."

✝✝✝
Chapter 25

Of course Mary had not mentioned to Brad anything about her experience at Bob's Dance Studio. But she had relayed the entire story to her best girlfriend, Jodi. She had been titillated by it, and urged her friend to go back. That's what Mary did the next week.

She had called Bob beforehand. He said he'd make sure they had a one-on-one session.

When she arrived, Bob looked spectacular. A skin tight leotard that offered a noticeable bulge at the crotch. Then a tight black T-shirt that clung to his large, taut biceps. And finally, the jet black hair, pulled back again into a ponytail. He greeted her with a friendly kiss on the cheek.

"How is my darling Mar – ie today?" he quipped, prolonging the name with a faux Italian accent.

"Perfecto, Roberto," she played back, rolling the "r's" in his name as she said it.

"Have you been practicing since we last met?" He asked.

"As much as I could. Of course I didn't have a pole to use. My husband hasn't installed one yet," she said with a smile.

"I can't imagine why not," Bob said with a return smile. And then in a conspiratorial whisper: "But I must confide, I know for a fact that most of my students don't tell their significant others about their time here."

"I think there's a reason for that, Bob," she said winking.

Mary went into the same room to change. And how everything had changed. This time she felt no embarrassment knowing that Bob was right outside the room. On the contrary, the thought made her slightly wet, her nipples to tauten against the synthetic fabric of her bra. She had brought an especially provocative outfit: tiny spandex shorts that advertised her small, round butt, and, compared to last time, an even smaller, clinging halter top. All black, to match Bob's. Or Roberto's, she mused.

When she exited, Bob was already beginning to warm up. She took her place next to him, and began stretching. On occasion, a part of their bodies would inadvertently touch – now a hand, then a leg. The sensation was hardly displeasing.

After about five minutes, Bob said, "Mary, do you remember any of the moves? Let's start with the basic Fireman, and then the Cross Front Hook. Just follow me."

Mary went to the nearest pole while Bob went to the one farther away, after first hitting the switch for the music.

She could watch him both directly and in the mirrors. Multiple images of beauty, she thought.

At home she had been clandestinely working out, and although pole-less, she found she could still practice some of the maneuvers holding on to one of the railings on her back porch. She just wanted to stay limber, and keep the muscle memory from her first time intact. So today she felt better prepared, being in good shape and more experienced.

They eased their way through the initial movements, Mary gaining more confidence with each passing minute. She also marveled again at the gracefulness Bob displayed during the dances, despite his muscularity. They continued with more difficult moves, working their way into an Attitude Heel, where Mary twirled around the pole with the heel of her right foot hooked on the pole above her head, and the Carousel, where she held the pole with both hands, placed her feet against the pole, and spun.

"Sweet Mary. You are incredible today! I've never had a student pick this up so fast. You are truly a natural," Bob exclaimed.

Mary did feel good about herself. Even better after Bob's accolades. She was also getting into the zone, the one she had entered for the first time last week: that sense of freedom, exhilaration, almost like she was flying. What did

Freud say about dreams of flying, she asked herself, quietly enjoying the thought. She became one with the pulsating music, the lights beating in rhythmic unison with the sound. She occasionally glanced at Bob's mastery of the dance, and listened to his well-timed but infrequent pointers: "Mary, don't grip the pole so tight," or "Control the spin with your feet."

After about forty-five minutes, Bob walked over and turned down the volume of the music. Mary was spent. Both of them glistened with sweat.

"Mary, let's rest and talk." Bob took her hand and led her to one of the couches set against the walls. They sat down, their bodies touching slightly, without the slightest feeling of discomfort. Mary was still lightly panting. Bob gave no indication of the exertion both had just undergone.

"I love watching your body move," he began. "You have such an innate, natural beauty. And such a fire in you. Your husband is very lucky."

A shadow of sadness passed quickly over her countenance.

"I'm so sorry Mary. Did I say something wrong?"

"No, Roberto. I'm the one to be sorry. What you said is so sweet, so nice. I just . . . well, never mind. You don't want to hear it." A tear began forming around her left eye. She wiped it off quickly.

"But Mary, I do. I do want to hear it," he said, as he gently took her hand in his. "Please, trust me enough for this. Anything you tell me will not leave this room. I swear it."

"Roberto. I already feel so close to you." She gently squeezed his hand. "But I don't want to burden our new friendship with my problems."

"It's no burden, Mary. Just the opposite. I feel it's a way for us to become even closer friends. Sometime I may need you to listen to my problems. We all have them, you know."

Their locked hands had fallen non-nonchalantly on his thigh. Then for only an instant, they brushed lightly against his crotch. She then noticed the huge bulge in his pants. The sight momentarily took her breath away. She was instantly turned on in a way she had never experienced. For a second she was afraid her wetness would appear on the fabric of her shorts and give her away.

Her voice came out in a whisper. "I'm just so lonely. My husband shows no interest in me. I don't like admitting this, but we haven't had sex in over a year. I'm going crazy. I also believe he must be having an affair. He's acting so strangely. Twice now I've caught him in the bathroom with a Victoria Secret catalog, and the Sports Illustrated swimsuit edition. I know men like to look at those things, but he seems fixated on them. Then there's the fact he won't touch me."

"My poor Mary," he said softly. "A bad marriage like that is Hell. I know because I've been through one. Tell me how I can help you."

She told him silently. Moving her hands directly over his hard cock. Then with her lips, kissing him madly on his mouth, his neck. Next, after pulling his leotard down, on his penis, his balls. Enjoying his sounds, his moaning. Slowly, carefully they began removing each others clothing, then frantically as they got down to the last pieces. He got his mouth between her legs, and gyrating his head, licked all around her vulva, paying special attention to her throbbing clit. Then lifting her up, his physical strength adding to her passion, he laid her over the end of the couch, and entered her from behind. His penis was hard as concrete, large and thick. As he pumped her hard, she went into a frenzy, her moaning becoming screams of delight. After what seemed like eons of pleasure, he came in a monstrous spurt, filling her to overflowing. He stayed in her for a minute, both of them out of breath, totally sated. They then lay together on the couch, their sweat intermingling, swimming together in it.

＋＋＋
Chapter 26

Martha looked down with horror. She instantly grasped what had happened. It was obvious. As she ran to the front door, she screamed at George to meet her outside at once. When she got to the area under Billy's bedroom window, Billy was just struggling to get up.

"Auntie. Help me. Please! I think I've broken something."

She responded by kicking him hard, in the ribs. "You fucking little bastard. This is how you reward me for taking care of you?"

Billy collapsed, writhing in pain. He was barely able to mutter, "Please Auntie. Please. I'll be a good boy."

By this time, George, clad only in his pajama bottoms, had arrived. It took him a little longer to understand what had happened. "Billy. Billy. Are you OK?"

Martha punched him in the arm. "Don't you dare coddle the boy. Don't you see what he's done? He sneaked out on us. Probably to visit that whore."

"I know Martha, but he may be hurt. Let's take a look at him."

Martha blocked his way, and grabbed Billy's arm to pull him up. Billy yelled again. She was small, but incredibly strong when she was incensed. Billy was just too heavy. She turned toward George with flashing hatred in her eyes: "Help me get him up, you worthless idiot. Grab his other arm. Now!"

George did what he was told. Somehow, together, they managed to get the moaning Billy back up to his room and on his bed.

"George, get the hammer and some ten penny nails from the garage," she ordered. Again George obeyed, while Martha kept a close eye on Billy. He wasn't going anywhere.

George returned quickly. "George, nail those windows shut. Put four nails in each. Don't break any glass while you're doing it. Make sure no one will be able to open 'em."

The windows were secured in a few minutes. Martha yelled back into the room as they were leaving: "If you ever try to escape again, we'll find you. You know we will. And we'll break every bone in your body that time."

Billy lay in bed whimpering. He had never broken a bone before, but he was sure his left elbow was now. It was swelling up tremendously, and threw off a constant, throbbing pain. His whole body also ached.

He had never seen his Auntie so mad. He knew he had been a very bad boy. What had gone through his mind to cause him to sneak out like that? Yet the sweet, tender moments with Maria were what sustained him right now. Although hurting beyond description, he accepted the pain as atonement for his sins. He deserved what he got.

The next morning the pain had subsided a bit, but the swelling kept him from bending his elbow at all. He was able to fashion a rough splint using a belt, covered with a pillow case, which helped somewhat. By ten o'clock, though, he was getting very thirsty, and somewhat hungry. His tongue was dry and starting to swell. By one o'clock the combination of his hunger, thirst and pain started to make him delirious. Billy began hearing knocks on his door, and each time he carefully got off his bed, delicately holding his arm, only to find the sound was a figment of his imagination. Several times he yelled out his Aunt and Uncle's names, certain they were just on the other side, and received no response. By five o'clock, he could not take it anymore. He stood by the door, and began kicking it, almost in a trance at this point. He tried to call out their names again, but his extreme thirst muffled the sound from his lips. How long he stood there banging on the door with his foot, he didn't know. Eventually he lay down next to the door, curled into a ball, and fell into a feverish sleep.

In what seemed an eternity, Billy was awakened by the sound of the lock turning. He thought he was dreaming. The door suddenly pushed against his body. He yelped in fright. George appeared around the edge of the door with his finger to his lips: "Shssh Billy. It's me. Quiet."

Billy rolled away from the door. He couldn't stand, or sit up. George had a tray which he set down on the nightstand.

"Uncle. Help me," Billy pleaded. "I can't get up."

George gently lifted Billy from under his arms and sat him up on the bed.

"Billy, I've brought you some food and water. And some aspirin. But you have to promise me you won't tell Martha. She'll kill me. And then you."

"Okay, Uncle. I promise. Thank you so much."

George left the room quietly, carefully locking the door behind him.

Billy had just taken his first drink of fluids, and a small

bite of the sandwich, when he heard Martha screaming from their room at the top of her lungs: "You bastard. You absolute bastard. What have you done?!"

ⵌⵌⵌ

Chapter 28

Sam was able to convince Henry to pay another visit to
Dr. Henderson. At least it meant a couple of hours out of the
office, with an excuse to stop for lunch and a beer. Not anything
that Henry would take lightly.

When Henderson took Sam's call to set up the meeting,
he was much friendlier, and told them to stop by that afternoon,
if they could. They could.

His office looked even messier, if that was possible.

"You asked me earlier about the nature of my study,"
Henderson started right in. "I want to tell you about it to dispel
any notion that what you've heard from the medical
establishment could in any way be tied to the leakage, assuming
there was one. My study concentrated on the effect of DMT as
an entheogen."

"Entheo what?" Sampson interjected. "Please Doctor, I'm
not up on the latest scientific terms." Henderson noticed the
trace of a smirk on Sam's lips.

"Mr. Sampson, entheogen is not, technically, a scientific
term. It's a neologism derived from two ancient Greek words:
Entheos, an adjective meaning 'full of God, inspired, possessed' –
in fact, it's where we get the English word 'enthusiasm' – and the

word *Genesthai*, which roughly translates as 'to come into being'. Thus an entheogen is a substance which causes a person to experience feelings of inspiration – often in a religious or spiritual manner. Another way of saying it is, an entheogen is 'that which causes God to be within an individual'."

Sampson appeared openly irritated. "Please Doctor, let's get to the point. What can this drug do if you ingest it? Is this stuff like the LSD the young kids took back in the hippie days?"

"I'm getting to that, sir. But I have to explain it in my own way. You do want to know about the substance, don't you?"

"Of course Dr. Henderson. Please continue." It was Pritchard who encouraged him to go on.

"I performed a double blind study on approximately five hundred participants. That's one, in case you don't know, where neither the subjects of the experiment nor the persons administering the experiment know the critical aspects of the experiment. It's used to guard against both experimenter bias and placebo effects."

"Yes, I've heard the term, Dr. Henderson." Henry was trying to recover some dignity. He didn't like being talked down to – which most people did anyway.

Henderson continued: "Because of that, I had one of my top research assistants at the time, who is now a scientist of some renown, actually conduct the study. I sorted the data and drew the ultimate conclusions."

"What was his name?" Henry inquired.

"Dr. Charles Hurlock. He's now at the Mayo Clinic."

"Haven't heard of him," Henry retorted.

"You're not in that circle, Mr. Sampson. I can assure you he performed the experiment professionally and ethically. We found that, indeed, DMT, when properly administered, is a powerful entheogen. All the participants reported mystical or other-worldly experiences. Some had very detailed near-death encounters; others met alien beings, and were even transported to new worlds; but most simply rose to a higher level of spiritual awareness. They reported being closer to, or understanding God in a way they had never experienced before. A small minority had very sexual – erotic might be a better word – episodes."

Sam Pritchard had listened respectfully and intently. But it was now his turn to butt in.

"Did your studies cover the effects of long-term exposure to DMT. Or was it all short term?"

"The latter," Henderson replied. "All of the participants were administered small doses, and no further doses were given for at least several days, sufficient time for their bodies to rid themselves completely of the DMT. Moreover, the project only extended for several months."

"I've also done some reading on the subject, Doctor. Were

you careful to screen everyone involved for any family history of schizophrenia or similar mental conditions? Because prior studies have indicated DMT can trigger latent psychological and mental problems."

"Of course we were Mr. Pritchard," Henderson responded testily. "We had each participant submit a detailed questionnaire which covered not only their family, but also their own history of any mental disease or illness."

Pritchard would not be easily diverted. "Yes, but Doctor, as many researchers have discovered, subjective disclosures by the participants are unreliable. Did you also perform objective, random checks of the information given you?"

"No, we did not. But as any scientist knows, you have to rely on some basic, foundational data to move the project ahead. Substantiating family or personal histories would have taken enormous resources, which I feel were better spent elsewhere."

"I hope that wasn't a serious mistake, Doctor Henderson," Sam stated.

Henry and Sam took their leave. As soon as he saw that the two men were out of earshot, Henderson closed and locked the door to his office. Pulling his personal phone book from the second drawer of his desk, he located the number he had not called in years, and one he had hoped he never would have to call again.

Sandoz answered on the second ring. "What are you calling me on this line for?" he screamed into the receiver. "I told you never to call me here again, damn it!"

"Settle down. Settle down!" Henderson's voice was guardedly raised now. He did not want anyone to hear him in this old, drafty building. "We've got to talk. Soon. And if not on the phone, then in person."

Sandoz knew what this was about. He had expected the call. A brief blurb on the discovery of the chemical leak had appeared ominously one day several months ago in the local paper. This one he couldn't overlook. Henderson was a loose cannon, and he had to control the situation.

"Fine, Richard. Why don't we meet at the Capitol tomorrow for lunch. I'm sure we can find a quiet corner to discuss whatever you want. But let's both agree not to talk to anyone about anything until we talk. Okay? How's one?"

"One is good. But just so you know, two guys from the Board of Health barged in on me a couple of weeks ago. I thought I had put them at ease. They called me recently and wanted to talk again, and I agreed because of how well the first meeting went. They just left. One of them is a young zealot, but the problem is he's smart. I'm not so sure what to think now."

"Second visit!?" Sandoz boomed. "When was the first? And why in the hell didn't you tell me about it?"

"Because I thought it was nothing. And I told them nothing. Except it was impossible that the shit could have gotten into the water supply. See ya tomorrow."

Chapter 29

The Capitol Grille was the best, and poshest restaurant in town. Of course, that wasn't saying much. The next candidate was the Ole English Pub, whose ersatz antique English interior, with its dim lighting and dark stained pine benches, bar, and panels, would depress anyone but the most stalwart drinkers.

Of course Sandoz would pick this place, Henderson thought as he pulled up to valet parking. Even after the bankruptcy, he came out smelling like a rose. People like him always did. Underpay your workers; condemn them to intolerable working conditions; pollute the environment; put the business in your wife's name to get minority status and pull every red cent out of it; and let the company collapse under the weight of the unpaid vendors, underfunded pension plans, and governmental sanctions. Henderson knew as a fact the chemical company was not the only enterprise Sandoz had owned that fit this bill. It was only the most recent and immediate.

Dr. Henderson walked in and asked the hostess if a Mr. Sandoz had left his name with her. He had, and she led him to a back booth that was well out of the mainstream of customers and waiters.

Sandoz looked much younger and fitter than he had

anticipated. A retirement full of leisure time, with plenty of ill-gotten gain as support, had set well with Harold. He was dressed in well-pressed slacks and a light green golf shirt. The tone of a deep tan was enhanced by his silver gray hair, recently cut.

"Hi Richard," Sandoz boomed confidently as he got up half-way to shake his hand. "It's been a long time. I'm sorry we've never gotten together in these six years. My fault, entirely."

Always the consummate politician, Richard thought.

"Nice to see you too, Harold. It has been a while. But I could have called too. The work of a professor and scientist never seems to cease. Maybe this will be the start of a new relationship."

"I hope it will. I certainly hope it will," Harold said, emphasizing the second "hope" with a heavy pat on Richard's back.

The two engaged in small talk for a few minutes: how the wives and kids were doing, the local sports teams. One would have thought they were the best of friends.

They ordered martinis: for Harold, Smirnoff, straight up with a twist; for Richard, an appletini, with Grey Goose. The same old pussy, Harold thought to himself. Also appetizers and a salad. Then the real talk began. Harold, as was his wont, took the initiative.

"I know what you called about, Richard. I read the article

in the paper. I haven't been out to the company site in years, and I don't intend to go there. But the trustee in the bankruptcy was supposed to handle all the clean-up. Everything. I washed my hands of the business just months after the trustee took over. So I don't know what happened, and frankly I don't care. The key is that we don't panic, don't go spilling off at the mouth, and everything will be okay."

"That's easy for you to say, Harold, but we could face some serious liability here if that crap actually got out. I mean, do you know what it does to people?"

"Let me correct you. I have no liability. The company stored the DMT. The company was responsible for its disposal. And you won't find my name anywhere in the corporate papers except as a member of the board of directors. Board members have no personal liability. I know that from personal experience."

Richard sensed Harold was bluffing here. He knew through the grapevine that the EPA, even the IRS, had been only a stone's throw from shutting down Mr. Sandoz for good on several occasions. Or locking him up.

"Well I don't know all the legal intricacies, but you assured me that the stuff would be properly disposed of. Now I find out the fucking tank was sitting out in a field to rust, and eventually burst open. And I'm getting visits from assholes from the health department. What am I supposed to tell them!" Henderson was almost screaming at this point.

"Quiet down, you idiot!" Sandoz said through gritted teeth. "What did I just say? If we're cool about this, nothing will happen. You tell them nothing. That's what you tell them. You don't know anything, except the results of your stupid little experiment. And by the way, I don't know what it does to people, because I haven't read anything you wrote about it. All I know is what you first told me, which is DMT is found naturally in all of us, is very mild, and doesn't pose a danger. Are you saying something else now?"

Richard wanted to lunge across the table and strangle the S.O.B. But he knew inwardly he was a coward, and had never, and would not now initiate a physical confrontation.

"What I told you, and you know it, is that DMT is not dangerous if controlled. That's what my research proved. That's also why I made it very clear to you that the remaining DMT had to be carefully destroyed. But if it did get into the Cary water supply – which I don't think it could have – I'm not sure what would happen. I've read no reports of that ever happening. I just don't want to be around if it's spreading throughout this community."

Chapter 30

That night Janna again had one of her dreams. One among many that had been disturbing her sleep as of late. She had been in some kind of accident. Bright lights shone down on her. She was in a hospital operating room. Masked surgeons and nurses hovered above her. They were shaking their heads, as if something had gone wrong. Janna felt no pain, but she sensed she was dying. Slowly the room, and everything in it receded into the distance. She was floating in a kind of blue-green ether. Behind her was an unimaginable and fearful blackness. Then a pinpoint of light appeared in what was now a shimmering fabric surrounding the ether. She yearned to reach the light beyond. Somehow she knew if she could just get there, tear open the fabric where the light appeared, she would be safe. If she didn't, the blackness would gradually absorb her. The thought terrified her. For in that blackness resided her worst thoughts and fears. She awoke with beads of perspiration settled on her brow.

She had not had the dreams for years – in fact, since she had gotten roped into that damn experiment. She had been in college. Needed money bad. There was this ad in the local newspaper. Seemed like really easy money. Just had to go to this place and live for a week. They told them half of them would be getting this mild experimental drug that would be used to cure depression. The other half would be administered a placebo. She knew she got the real thing when, first, she settled into a beautiful, generalized state of euphoria. For days. But then the nightmares came. The doctors, or whoever they were, were very interested in the content of the dreams. She left the experiment early. Didn't even get paid. She just couldn't take what was happening to her at night. Horrible things. Fortunately they went away as soon as she got away from the drug. Until now.

Janna needed to speak with her father about both her dreams, and her waking thoughts. Sometimes she could not discern the difference between them. She found him in his study.

"Daddy, can I speak with you for a few minutes? It's important."

"Sweetheart, I'm kind of busy right now."

"Please Daddy!"

His daughter's insistence at this early hour in the morning took Dan by surprise. He usually didn't hear or see her and Britney until noon on a weekend. "Okay Honey. What is it?"

"I had one of my terrible dreams last night. They're coming back again. I'm also having the bad thoughts."

The pastor's memory instantly went back to that day, over six years ago, when he and Helen sat before the doctor in his office and heard him explain that, after all the tests, he had to confirm that Janna suffered from a mild form of schizophrenia. It was very treatable. The medications they had now could allow her to lead a fairly average life. Dan next heard a disembodied voice, then realized it was his own. "But Dr. Willis. I don't understand. How could this happen so quickly? Janna was always such a well-adjusted child. She was valedictorian of her high school senior class. Had been doing very well in college. Dean's List each of her first three years. I just don't understand." He was sobbing quietly at this point, and could barely get the words out. Helen looked shell-shocked. Disbelieving.

It had started about nine months before that fateful meeting with Dr. Willis. They had received a series of phone calls from Janna's roommate. She was concerned. Janna was not getting up in the morning. Was skipping her classes. This was totally unlike her. When Dan or Helen tried to call her, she was largely unavailable, and when she would talk to them, she sounded lethargic, out of it.

At first, they were sure it was a spiritual battle. They had been aware Janna was dating a boy they hadn't met, and she had confided to her mother that she was sleeping with him. They urged her to cease sinning, and to pray and read her Bible daily.

Eventually they got a call from her guidance counselor. Janna was failing all of her courses, primarily because she was not turning in assignments or attending classes. Then came the medical visits: first to find a physiological cause, which ultimately turned into a battery of psychological tests. Now here they were, hearing the words they feared the most. Dan was still not sure the Devil wasn't involved.

"Janna. Have you been taking your medications? Or called Dr. Willis? How long has this been going on?"

"Just a couple of months Daddy. I have been taking my meds. I didn't want to call Dr. Willis until I saw if it passed on its own. But I really feel now I have to talk to him."

"What have the bad thoughts been all about?" As if he didn't know. Paranoid delusions, for sure.

"I'm getting so angry at Elaine. She has such a perfect child. She's always rubbing that in my face. I also think Hanna has been making fun of Britney when they're together. It's very subtle. Britney doesn't even realize it. But I know. I don't want Britney's self-esteem to be permanently damaged."

"Are you sure about this, Honey? You know the bad thoughts aren't usually accurate. I've never noticed anything when Hanna and Britney are together. Granted, I don't see them very often. Is this something that could be only in your mind? Have you prayed over it?"

Janna stood up suddenly, almost knocking over the chair she had been sitting on. Her face was beet red, and her lips trembled with rage. "How dare you Daddy. How dare you! In my mind?! Guess I'm going to have to handle this my own way!"

Janna ran up to her bedroom and smothered her shrieks in her pillow.

✝✝✝
Chapter 31

Dr. Willis was a tough man to reach, much less get an appointment with. But when Pastor Dan described the situation to his secretary, she was able to put him in sooner because of a recent cancellation.

Dan had been to the office many times, but not in some time. It was in a professional office building in the center of town. Dan respected the Doctor, but he always saw him with a sense of foreboding. It was rarely good news.

He arrived on time, and was shown to a chair in the office almost instantly, a rarity indeed. Dan thought immediately that the Doctor had aged noticeably since his last visit. He was still a handsome man, but the gray had fully overtaken his once salt and pepper scalp and beard. The lines on his face had become craggy.

"Hi Dan. Good to see you again. How long has it been?" It was apparent the respect was mutual.

"Good to see you too, Doctor," Dan said with as much enthusiasm as he could muster. "I think it's been at least a couple of years."

"At least. I saw Janna last year about this time," Dr. Willis said as he checked the file notes in front of him. "How about the church? Everything going well there?"

"Oh, yes. Attendance is up. And the giving is stayin' right with it. Not that that's so important," the Pastor said with a sparkle in his eyes.

"Good. Glad to hear it. But I guess we're here to discuss Janna, right? At least that's what Beatrice told me," Dr. Willis said, nodding toward his reception area.

Dan shifted slightly in his chair. "Yes, Doctor. I'm concerned. She's been acting peculiarly lately. She said she's been taking her medications, and I have no reason to disbelieve that."

"I think she has too," the Doctor cut in. "I've spoken to her several times on the phone over the past several months, and I've gotten pretty good at assessing a patient's credibility on that issue. She reported no suicidal ideation, or that she was hearing voices. I think we'd see something like that if she was off her medicine."

"Well, what I've noticed recently is quite different from her prior symptoms. First, it's her language. If I didn't know any better, I'd say my daughter has come down with a sudden case of Tourette Syndrome. I was unaware she even knew some of the four letter words that have come out of her mouth recently."

"Has she manifested any other symptoms of Tourette? Like facial, or body tics?"

"No, I haven't seen those. It's all the outbursts of foul language."

"That technically is called coprolalia. It's associated with the exclamation of obscene words or socially inappropriate and derogatory remarks. Without the physical manifestation of tics, I'm doubtful it's actually Tourette."

"Copro . . . what? Doctor, I'm not familiar with that word. How do you spell it?"

"C...O...P...R...O...L...A...L...I...A. It comes from the Greek words 'kopros', meaning 'faeces', and 'lalia', to 'talk'. I'm sure you get the drift of that. I don't remember anything in her history that would cause a sudden change in speech like that," Willis said with some concern in his voice. "I always found her to be polite and respectful, even at her worst moments."

"She always had been. Plus you know that our religious beliefs don't allow for that kind of talk. The second thing is, the old paranoia is coming back, but this time with a twist. She's convinced that a good friend of hers and her daughter are ganging up on Britney. You know, teasing her and such. I've just never seen that happen, and I've been there when the two little girls have played together."

"You're sure there's no indication of that at all?" Dr. Willis interjected. "Have you been around them frequently enough to tell?"

"I believe I have," the Pastor replied. " Not only that, she's been preoccupied with this thought that the Devil is working on her. Trying to get her to do things she wouldn't otherwise do. I think you know we believe the Devil is real – that he's out there, in person – tempting all of us to stray from the path of righteousness. But I fear Janna is obsessed with the idea. A couple of young ladies from Janna's bible study – she's teaching it now on Sunday mornings – have told me the last two classes have been dedicated to Satan. Janna has also confided to the girls that she's worried what the Devil is doing to her."

"Could this just be a reflection of her beliefs, Pastor? You yourself said that you believe Satan is real. I assume that goes for Janna as well. Maybe she's interpreting her paranoia as an instrument of the Devil, and not her illness. I disagree with that, of course, but at least it's consistent. I know you had a problem believing her illness was just that – something treatable by medication and analysis – rather than a spiritual battle between the forces of good and evil, remediable by prayer only."

"Doctor, I believe God gives the power to heal to physicians. So anything beneficial to cure sickness comes directly from God. And, yes, I also think there's a war going on out there. We can't see it, except in our behavior. So at the same time that disease may attack us, the Evil One will be there as well, as a source of discouragement, of hopelessness."

Willis listened intently. He was going to break in, but allowed Dan to continue:

"I think my concerns are also based on what I've observed in the church. You had asked me how things were going. I talked about attendance, about giving. But I didn't mention some other events that have bothered me a great deal. For one, we discovered that a well-respected member of our body – probably the last person I would expect to do something like this – had a personal blog that contained some outrageous material. Very scatological."

"We may have something in common here. I do think that the internet is the work of the Devil," Doctor Willis said with an expression that imparted some tone of jest, some of seriousness.

"Yes, I think we agree there," Dan responded. "But there's more. I celebrated the Holy Eucharist at the church last week. It's something we've done two times a year for decades."

"That's where you take of the bread and wine, believing they represent the body and blood of Jesus?" Doctor Willis inquired.

"Yes, in a way. It goes a little farther than that, however. We actually believe that the bread and wine *become* the body and blood. In any event, as I said, we've performed the rite scores of times. It's a sacred rite, so we take it seriously. It's done solemnly, with dignity. The time last week – the time I'm referring to – the ceremony got totally out of hand."

"What do you mean, 'out of hand', Pastor?"

"Well, it proceeded normally for a while. And it's

true that I felt I gave a powerful introduction to it. I wanted our church to rise to a higher spiritual plane, especially in light of what we found out about the one constituent I just mentioned – the one with the website – but also because I'd been concerned about the general spiritual laxity in the church. Possibly even Janna's situation entered into the picture. I tell you Doctor, I've never seen anything like it in my twenty-five years as a pastor."

Doctor Willis shifted uneasily in his chair. "Like what, Dan? You're starting to scare me now."

"Let me finish. It started with a murmuring amongst the congregation. Almost a buzzing. The sound grew louder and louder, until I realized it was the noise of everyone – and I mean everyone – in the church praying out loud, which has never happened before. Then a number of people began speaking in tongues, some even laying prostrate on the floor as they moaned and writhed."

"I think I've heard of 'speaking in tongues'," the Doctor said. "What exactly does that mean?"

"The technical, non-Christian name for it is Glossolalia. Glossolalia is believed by many Christians to have come into the Christian experience in the first century on the day of Pentecost after the Crucifixion of Jesus. It comes from a passage in the Bible. Acts Ch. 2 says: ' … there appeared unto them cloven tongues like as of of fire … divided unto all of the individuals in the upper room.' They were said to speak in 'unknown tongues as the spirit gave them utterance'. The book of Acts is found in the New Testament immediately after the Gospel of John and is considered to be the story of the very early church. The act of speaking in tongues is supposed to be a continuing sign, or miracle, if you will.

"Most churches, including ours, do not practice the act. That's why it was so bizarre when many in our congregation simultaneously started doing it. I know for a fact most, if not all of them had never spoken in tongues in their lives. It was completely spontaneous. I lost control of the congregation soon thereafter. I shouted for everyone to calm down, to take their seats – many times I did that – but to no avail. I simply walked out because I could not stand to witness any longer what was happening. It was of the Devil, not of God, in my opinion."

"What ultimately happened, then. How did it come out?" Willis asked.

"I understand in talking with people that it took several hours. Finally, one by one, people quieted, and left."

The two men sat in silence for several minutes – not uncomfortably – but in their own deep thoughts.

Dr. Willis spoke up first: "What you have just told me about Janna; about the member with the website; about the service last week; has troubled me greatly. Especially in light of what I'm about to tell you. But first you must promise me that what we discuss here will be strictly confidential – that neither of us will disclose our discussions to others. Is that agreed?"

"I just assumed it would be," Dan replied. "I know I'm not seeing you formally as a patient – and maybe I should have prefaced my remarks with the same understanding – I wouldn't want what I just said to get out either. So it's agreed."

"Good. I have become increasingly concerned by what I have witnessed in my professional capacity. I can best summarize it like this: over the past several months, the sickest of my clientèle – those with serious mental illnesses, such as schizophrenia, like Janna, or manic depression – have definitely gotten sicker. There's a greater report of hallucinations, hearing voices, etc. I've had to increase their dosages significantly. In addition, I've also seen a dramatic rise in first time clients. Whereas before I may have been contacted by a dozen potential new clients a year, I've been approached by that many in the past two months. And these are people who have reported to me that they've never seen a psychiatrist before in their lives, and yet they're experiencing serious symptoms. It concerned me so much I actually reported it to the Board of Health, which I've never done before."

Pastor Dan listened intently, and again both sat quietly for a minute once Willis had finished.

"This is all very disturbing," Dan said. I don't know what to make of it. Of course, my initial reaction is to take a spiritual approach on it. See it through the filters of my religious upbringing. Conclude that this is truly the work of Satan – that somehow He has chosen this time, this place, to work incredible evil. But I also have too much respect for your profession to exclude the possibility of a psychological component to it."

"And you know that I have to view reality through the lens of my upbringing, my education, my profession," Dr. Willis responded. But even with that said, I cannot lose this uneasy feeling I have – in the core of my being – that something else is going on here. All I hope is that we get to the bottom of it quickly. I fear it's going to get worse before it gets better."

With that, the men took their leave.

✚ ✚ ✚

Chapter 32

Brad wasted no time in setting up the apparatus to administer the drug to Vanessa. He kept up a steady banter, wanting to keep her at ease. Where was she working now? A veterinarian's assistant? Isn't the medical field fascinating? And so on. Miss Shaw was fine until he placed the mask over her face, when she exhibited some momentary panic. Brad was able to settle her by removing the mask and placing it on himself to show her how to breathe slowly. When he reapplied it, she was smiling. She didn't know, of course, that he had doubled the normal dosage.

Brad watched as she slowly went under. When he was sure she was completely unconscious, he walked over and gently, so as not to make any sound, clicked the doorknob button to the locked position. Next he went to the recessed speaker in the wall that carried the mood music that was distributed throughout the office, and turned up the volume.

Slowly, as if it were a mantra, he began repeating Vanessa's name, "Vanessa … Vanessa … Vanessa …" as he carefully undressed, hanging his clothing fastidiously on the hooks on the back of the door. Then, again, as if in slow motion, he gently untied the strings of her johnny, and pulled the edges of the gown back. Vanessa was now fully exposed before him. Brad shuddered with expectation. His erection was enormous.

Using some petroleum jelly, he prepared her for his entry. Laying on top of her, he lifted her legs back, so her knees almost touched her head, and slipped in easily. His pelvis instinctively began to thrust, harder and harder, faster and faster. He was now in a frenzy. His long pent-up frustration fueled his desire. He was vaguely aware of a momentary concern that the copulation sounds would alarm his staff. Finally he erupted in a frothy paroxysm, and lay, totally spent, spread across Miss Shaw's body.

His reverie was harshly interrupted by her intense choking. She was grabbing madly at the mask, trying to disengage it from her face. He quickly lifted himself off of her, afraid his weight had forced the air out of her lungs. But she still gasped for air, repetitively, as he tried to control her flailing arms. Horrible gurgling sounds were now emanating from her throat. Fearful even more now that the noises would alert his employees to the danger within the room, he covered her mouth with his hand as best he could to stop them.

He didn't know how long he stayed in that position, his fingers clamped around her lips. All sense of the passage of time was lost. All he cared about was that she was now silent. The fact that she was no longer breathing simply escaped him. It wasn't until he had cleaned her vagina of the emission, and tied the johnny back around her, that he became aware of her condition. Now he was in total panic mode. He immediately began mouth to mouth resuscitation. After several minutes, he was hyperventilating, and making no progress. Brad stopped and looked at her, feeling for a pulse.

Vanessa Shaw was now quite dead.

✟✟✟
Chapter 33

Mary drove home in a state of delightful delirium. She had never experienced sex like that. Ever. By the time she reached her house, her resolve was firmly entrenched. She was going to tell her husband she wanted a divorce. The years of frustration, of being unloved, exploded to the surface. But why wait? She wanted to get the job done now.

She backed out of the driveway and headed for Brad's office. She didn't care if he had a patient, or if the office staff was present. In fact, she didn't just want a divorce – she wanted him out of the house today.

She barged into the office and went right by Susan, the receptionist, on her way to her husband's examining room. Susan offered a slight protest: "Mrs. Wilson. The Doctor is in with a patient. Let me buzz him for you."

Mary would not be deterred. She went to the door and was surprised to find it locked. She rattled it a few times, and then gave the door a couple of loud slaps with the palm of her hand. An angry voice responded from within:

"What!? I told you I was not to be disturbed. I'll be out in a minute!"

"Brad, I need to talk to you – now!"

"Mary – is that you? What are you doing here? I'm in the middle of an examination. Is there anything wrong?"

"What's wrong is our marriage. I demand to speak with you at once." She gave the door a few more whacks, but this time with her fist. Out of the corner of her eye she caught the concerned look of Susan, who had moved from behind the reception desk.

A moment later, the door knob turned and she heard the pop of the push lock. As she looked up, she caught the left half of her Husband's face as he peered around the crack in the door. The sight terrified her. The one eye she could see was wild, crazed. Sweat dripped down his reddened jaw. He said in a hoarse whisper: "OK, my darling. Come in. Come in."

Chapter 34

Billy wolfed down the food and water as quickly as he could. The sudden ingestion almost made him vomit. He heard a crashing sound down the hall from the direction of his aunt and uncle's room. Then shattering glass. George yelped in a muffled tone. Billy quietly, but carefully so as not to bang his throbbing elbow, slid under his bed. After about five minutes, he heard the lock turn. From his vantage point under the bed, he could just barely see the door slowly open. He held his breath. Next came the slippered feet of his aunt. Shuffling slowly toward the bed. She stopped by the edge. Then silence for a few seconds.

"Billy ... Billy," she uttered in a low monotone. "Billy. Where are you? Come out wherever you are." Then a contemptuous laugh. "I know where you are, stupid boy. Think you can hide from me? You can never hide from auntie."

Billy next saw a hand reaching under the bed. Then he felt a sharp, pricking pain in his side. Then the glint of something metallic. She had a large kitchen knife, and was stabbing at him! Billy crammed himself as far as he could against the wall on the far side of the bed. He could feel the blood trickling down the side of his stomach.

"Auntie! Stop! Please stop!" He pleaded. Still she swept

her hand under the bed, the blade just inches from his body. Billy could hear George whimpering in the background: "Martha. Please. You're gonna kill the boy. Then what'll we do? Please!"

The hand paused. Billy could now see the clear outline of the knife George used to carve the turkey at Thanksgiving. It was huge. And very sharp. Once more she poked at him, and the tip broke the skin just above his right hand as he tried to ward off the blow.

"Ow!" He screamed. "Auntie, you're hurting me. Stop!"

Slowly the hand disappeared from view. He heard Martha stand up.

"George," she hissed. "Take him down to the basement and chain him to the soil pipe. Do it now, or I'll kill you both right now. Right in this room."

George came over to the bed and put his head under. "Billy. Let's go now. I think she'll let us go if we do what she says. Come on." He extended his hand. Billy grabbed it, and George pulled him from under the bed. Billy kept his eyes riveted apprehensively on Martha.

They made their way to the door, making a wide berth around Martha, who just stood there, shaking and glowering, with the knife down by her side. Billy was not bleeding badly from his two wounds, but enough to leave little droplets of blood to mark his path down the stairs.

The basement was unfinished, poorly lit,and wet. Billy had hated to go down there for any reason. Now to his horror he saw that a chain was looped around the thick, cast iron pipe that led to the septic system. Hanging from the end of the chain was a pair of handcuffs. Where had they come from, Billy wondered in a daze?

George led Billy over to the chain, placed the handcuffs over his wrists, and locked them in place. These are no kid's, play handcuffs, Billy thought. The chain was just long enough to allow Billy to sit with his back against the stone wall, but not to fully lay down. The floor was cold and damp.

"Uncle George, can you ask Martha if I can have some water, and a band aid for my cuts?" Billy pleaded.

George glanced up the stairs toward the basement door, and then whispered. "I will Billy. I'm sorry about this. I don't know what's gotten into her. Let's not rock the boat and see if she settles down. Okay?"

Billy sat there, bleeding, his elbow in severe pain, chained to the pipe. As he watched George slowly trudge up the stairs, he glimpsed Martha's shadow slowly passing by the door.

⫟ ⫟ ⫟
Chapter 35

Billy had no concept of how long he had been down there. Sleep had come only sporadically, restlessly, during the night. His wrists were red and sore from the times his body literally hung from the pipe as he slept. A little daylight crept through the small, single window at the other end of the cellar. He shivered from the damp cold.

I must have really been bad, he thought. I guess I deserve this. Auntie wouldn't do it if I didn't. I've got to try to be better. Then I know she'll let me out. I'll promise her I'll never go outside until she says it's okay. I won't ever go to see Maria again. She'll understand. It's better to be obedient.

But Billy never got the chance to tell Martha anything. She didn't come down again. George brought a little food and water twice a day, and removed the cuffs once each day so Billy could use the bucket which festered next to him. George wouldn't speak to him, even when Billy pleaded with him to tell Martha he was sorry; that it would never happen again; that he would be a good boy from now on.

That day passed, and then the next, and then another. Billy's wrists became bloody, the pain from them almost unbearable. His thighs and crotch were raw and chafed from the times he had to urinate at night in his pants. Even his own smell was more than he could stand. George started coming down only once a day, still deaf to Billy's increasingly plaintive cries that he'd do better, he was sorry.

Slowly, an instinctual will to survive began to take over. He knew he'd die down there if he didn't do something. The pipe he was chained to seemed unbreakable. It was a good six inches in diameter, solid cast iron. On the fourth day he found he could twist his wrists, as painful as it might be, and grab the chain with both hands. This not only relieved the pressure on his wrists, but enabled him to exert some force, and apply his weight, against the pipe. He could also maneuver the chain so it lay directly over a joint in the pipe. For hours he heaved against the chain, also employing a sawing motion on the surface of the pipe. Once or twice he thought he felt a little give in the pipe, but then realized it was probably just the flexion in his hands. He fell asleep exhausted from the effort, every bone in his body aching.

Billy was haunted by terrible nightmares all night. In one a legion of sharp-toothed rats approached him, spread out across the width of the basement, slowly moving toward him in the dark, their pink tongues flicking at the air. In another, a horrible, deformed old lady crept down the stairs, the meat cleaver she held in her hand glinting from the moon light filtering through the window. In both, he awoke screaming, drenched in sweat, his lips parched and dry.

When he awoke in the morning, he could not keep a normal string of thoughts connected in his head. Now, more than ever, he knew he was facing a prolonged, torturous death if he could not escape his shackles. With renewed strength, brought on solely by his desperation, he yanked at the chains, bringing all his strength and weight to bear against the pipe. Over and over again he thrust against it, until he could bear no more.

Sobbing with frustration, not able to last another minute in this God-forsaken prison, he looked around for some instrumentation to end his life. Billy had never contemplated suicide before this: now it was an act of mercy, to be desired, not feared. He saw a small shard of concrete that had fallen out of a chink in the stone foundation. It looked sharp. If he could just reach it, he could probably saw far enough into the veins in his wrists to bleed out. He reached for it, but it was still inches from his outstretched fingers. He lunged once, twice, then three times toward the weapon, to no avail. He summoned the stamina for one more try. With a final bust of energy, he threw himself at the concrete piece. Just at that moment, the soil pipe gave way with a sharp crack, spewing pieces of excrement everywhere, including Billy. He fell against the basement floor, the handcuffs and chain laying loosely at his side.

Chapter 36

Mandy had just finished her review of the property tax records at the Assessor's office when her cell started buzzing. She had set it to vibrate so as not to disturb those around her in the government office. She checked the caller ID, and answered immediately when she saw it was Sam.

"Hey Baby," she cooed softly, more to stimulate his sex glands than to keep from bothering others. "How's it shakin'?"

"Hi Mandy-kins. Goin' good here. Just got off the phone with that corporate lawyer in England. That's where Henderson set up most of his dummy corporations to run his research projects — together with the Cayman Islands, as we already knew. You really owe him a favor. He put a lot of work into this."

"Anything good?"

"Yes. It's very complicated. The shareholders of the corporations were a series of trusts. They're called 'nominee' trusts, I think he said. It's a well-known way to try to disguise the true controller of the trust, because the trust only names a trustee, but no beneficiaries. But the Trustee has no independent power except as dictated by the beneficiaries - whom we don't know."

"I've run into those trusts in my real estate courses. Also

my estate planning classes. Very clever."

"Simon – the attorney – well, I guess over there, it's Barrister, said he found a common thread woven through the documents. All of the named persons – again, mostly trustees of the trusts, directors and officers of the corporations, not beneficiaries or shareholders – had the same last name, Sandoz. There was a Helen Sandoz, Darren Sandoz, and a Darlene as well."

"That's odd. Was he able to find out anything about them?"

"Well, I was."

"You, Sherlock?" Mandy taunted him.

"Look Dr. Watson. You're not the only brainiac in this family, ya know?" Sam played along gently.

"Alright, alright. What 'cha find out?"

"It seems that the three Sandoz's I mentioned are the wife and two children of a Harold Sandoz, who actually lives in this area, a few counties over. Darlene Sandoz, according to the state records, is only fourteen years old. When I mentioned all this to Simon, he said he knew the name Harold Sandoz. Apparently there had been a significant investigation by Interpol in Europe into his business operations. He was never charged, but there were rumors of a large pay-off to some very influential people. That's all he knew about him at this time."

"Sandoz ... Sandoz," Mandy repeated. "I know that name. I bet if we searched the society pages of the Daily Telegraph we'd see a lot of them."

"The name doesn't ring a bell to me. But I've sure got some questions for Henderson. He's a lot deeper into this than I thought. What did you find out."

"Not a whole lot on my end. There's no property in the state owned directly by Dr. Henderson. But a Lucille Henderson is the record owner for a number of properties – several assessed for over a million dollars. One of those looks like his personal residence. No doubt that's his wife."

"Or fourteen year old daughter," Sam quipped.

"So assuming that's his wife, he's accumulated some significant assets for being a college professor. Do you want me to go any farther?"

"No. Why don't I have a little chat with Dr. Henderson again. See what I can find out from him."

"Okay, Honey, but be careful. There's something about this whole matter that's got me a little worried."

"Me too. Goodbye sweetie."

"Bye."

Chapter 37

Sam decided that there was no time like the present time. He dialed Dr. Henderson's office number. Surprisingly, he answered on the first ring.

"Henderson here."

"Dr. Henderson, this is Sam Pritchard again. How are you?"

There was an uneasy pause on the other end. "I'm all right. What can I do for you? I'm very busy right now."

"I just need a few minutes of your time. Could I come over now and talk with you?"

"I've got classes, staff meetings, conferences, all day. Plus I've told you everything I know."

"Well, I'm not so sure. Do you know a Harold Sandoz?"

Now a longer pause. "I think I've heard the name. Why do you ask?"

Sam gave him a brief primer on what he had learned. Leaving out some details.

"That's all very interesting. I don't know the other Sandoz' you mentioned. Maybe you should contact them."

"I intend to. Just thought I'd run it by you first. Sorry to bother you." Sam was dead certain Henderson was lying through his teeth.

After getting off the phone with Sam, Henderson immediately called Sandoz.

"Harold. We've got a bit of a problem here."

"Look Henderson. How many fuckin' times do I need to tell you this. You never call this number from one of your phones. What about that don't you understand?"

"You need to know this now," Henderson retorted. "Just got a call myself from that young health inspector. He knows everything. Well, almost everything. I don't know how he did it, but he did. He's got your name somehow. And Helen's. And the kids. Knows they're tied into the European deal."

"How could this happen? You assured me there was no way I could be connected. Now you say a local bureaucrat has discovered it. What the fuck is this?"

"I just wanted to let you know right away. I've got to go now, but we'll talk soon."

╬ ╬ ╬
Chapter 38

Sandoz had misgivings about Henderson from the beginning. He was a brilliant, but conniving scientist, no doubt. Yet Sandoz recognized a weakness in the man. He should know; Sandoz had been preying on the weaknesses of men since he could remember.

The realization was almost a coming of age for him. He was seventeen when an older woman told him of that moment in her life when she saw how her sexuality affected men – but more importantly, how she could manipulate men through her sexuality. She had been doing it successfully ever since. The conversation had taken place in one of her three homes worldwide – this one in Los Angeles, the others in Buenos Aires and Rome. After three lucrative divorces, of course.

With incredible clarity, Sandoz realized if he just read the signs – the tone of voice, the facial expressions – and thought hard about what the other man wanted and what his soft spots were, in most cases he had the edge. And a little edge would get you a long way.

Henderson's concept had been brilliant. Set up a bunch of dummy corporations around the world whose apparent purpose was to conduct legitimate research on DMT's effects on different peoples and cultures. It had been clearly shown that those effects depended much on the environmental conditions in which the participants were placed. But it was also clear that DMT had a popular, street demand. It was an hallucinogen, but without the nasty side effects of LSD or pscilicybin. There had been no reported cases of suicide, for example, with DMT, as there had been with the others. They found with a little experimentation that they could package the DMT in innocuous forms and distribute it from the new companies through a network of starving grad students who were happy to make a few dollars and party with the stuff themselves. Sandoz had been able to overlook Henderson's idiosyncrasies as the profits poured in.

Things went well for several years until the inevitable occurred: snitches arose from the ranks, and the authorities became suspicious. Sandoz responded simply by closing the companies and having them declare bankruptcy, sometimes all in one week.

Sandoz' name had never been attached to the enterprise. Only Henderson knew of his complicity. Sandoz had trusted him with the secret when things were going well. But now Henderson was a serious, potential liability.

Even more disturbing was this young Turk, Sam Pritchard. Sandoz knew the type – crusaders until they got old enough to take the money instead. He'd deal with Pritchard in due course.

Every successful man, at times, needed muscle. It could be his own: that's why tall, large men made it in this world easier than short, small ones. But more often it was someone else — especially when you were one of the short, small ones, like Sandoz. Sandoz had his man — he had met him in his early twenties, and used him ever since. A man who was at heart truly a bully. It was almost as if the cash didn't matter. Mike had been perfect. Anytime Sandoz needed to put a scare into an opponent — a competitor, a deadbeat who owed him money — he could call Mike and the problem would be taken care of. Often Sandoz knew nothing of the details. He just paid the money and savored the results.

That's why this next call was to Mike. He had briefly discussed the Dr. Henderson issue with him a few months back. As was their usual procedure, Sandoz left his number on Mike's pager; Mike would then go to the nearest pay phone and call him back. It was expected Sandoz would take his call, no matter what. Mike had made that quite clear one time when he showed up at Sandoz' office when Sandoz had not answered, despite their agreement that should never occur. Mike was huge, and very intimidating. He yelled down the hallway for Sandoz to come out, he needed to talk. It took a lot of explaining to his staff to pass that one off.

This time Sandoz was ready when Mike called back.

"Hey big guy. What's going on?"

"You called me, dirt-bag. Remember?" Mike was never one to coddle.

"Of course I did. Does that mean we can't exchange pleasantries? What side of the bed did you wake up on today?"

"It's been a tough day," Mike explained. "Had to get a little rough with some fuck-heads who've been avoidin' me. They got what was comin' to them, though."

"Hard day at the office, huh?" Sandoz quipped. Silence on the other end.

"Okay. Okay. Here's the deal. You know that Dr. Henderson I've told you about . . . ?"

"That friggin' fag,"Mike interrupted. "Hope this is about me bustin' him good. Always knew he'd be trouble."

"Relax Mike. Let me do the talking. I just need to put a little scare into him. I'm afraid he's going to spill his guts on something ... well ... uh ... delicate. It won't take much, as you know. Gotta let him know it'll be worse dealing with us than with the other people he thinks he might need to talk to. Can you handle this?"

"With pleasure. What's his address again?"

Sandoz told him, and then added: "I'll probably have one more for you soon. An easy one. A stupid health inspector. Young wimpy guy as far as I can tell. I'll let you know on that one."

"Fine. But what's his name?"

"Sam Pritchard. Lives here in town. But don't do anything until I tell you."

"No problem, boss. I'll take care of it. You'll get the bill in the mail," Mike said with a snigger in his voice.

Chapter 39

A talk with her father led Janna to agree to let Hanna play with Britney again. One more time. Elaine had already called her to try to set it up; Janna only had to acquiesce. Not too difficult.

Elaine dropped Hanna off around noon the next Saturday. Janna was going to take the girls to Burger Queen, and then do a little shopping for Britney. Elaine was kind enough to leave her with a twenty to buy a little something for Hannah as well.

BQ's went well. The girls were obviously happy to see each other, and talked incessantly throughout the meal. Janna was on the lookout for any aspersions Hanna might cast Britney's way, but there was nothing. Janna involuntarily let her guard down for a while.

Maybe it was the more familiar setting of the rectory. Or maybe the fact that she hated the cramped, close space of the small house. But almost immediately upon their return home, Janna began to pick up the hidden innuendos, the not so disguised barbs that Hanna was throwing at her daughter. She was a very clever little girl, Janna thought, but not too clever for her. She was onto her.

When they were playing Chutes and Ladders, Hanna's

laugh was more a witch-like cackle when Britney caught a chute and had to descend to a lower level. And her shrill cries of delight were too much to bear when Hanna hit a ladder and jumped ahead of Britney. It really took the cake when Hanna, with a triumphant "I won! I won!" got to the last square ahead of her daughter.

Janna was in the kitchen adjacent to the living room where the girls were playing. She was making them a peanut butter and jelly sandwich. Bad thoughts were swirling through her head. How can I get Hanna out of here? How can I make her disappear. I can't take much more of this torture.

A fly buzzed around her once and landed close by as she was preparing the food. Janna instinctively swatted it with a rolled-up newspaper laying on the counter. Squashed it good. Like I would like to squash Hanna, she mused. Without giving it a second thought, Janna picked up the dead fly by its wing, its guts drooling out of its body, and mixed it in with the jam of Hanna's sandwich. This will teach the little bitch!

Janna smiled coldly as she watched the girls eat. For a moment Janna was filled with dread that Hanna would choke on the insect, would feel its tiny legs crunch, taste the bitterness. But Hanna showed no indication she sensed anything was wrong. Maybe she is a little witch, Janna thought. She eats insects, and rodents too. So of course she wouldn't notice anything amiss.

-143-

From that moment on, every word, every action of Hanna's, convinced Janna more and more that Hanna was truly a witch. Hanna had powers she had never imagined, she now saw. She even seemed to be able to get Britney to laugh when she wanted her to, to play a new game when she wanted. It was as if Hanna now controlled her daughter's mind, thoughts, actions.

This is clearly the work of the Devil, Janna knew. She had heard her father preach about it. Satanism, witchcraft, they were all the same. Janna had allowed Satan himself to enter her house, play with her child! She stormed into the living room. "Hanna! Get your things together. You've got to go home now." Hanna looked shocked. Britney complained loudly. "Mom. She just got here. We were having so much fun. Let her stay a little while longer."

It took all of Janna's self-control to keep from grabbing the little witch by her arm and hauling her to her feet. Instead, she picked up Hanna's jacket, headed for the door, and said firmly: "Hanna. Come with me now. Britney, you stay here." Hanna dutifully got up and went out to the car.

How was she going to do this? Crash head on into an oncoming car? No, then she might be seriously hurt. Take her out to a remote area and bash her head in with a rock? A possibility. She just knew she had to do something. Now. It didn't matter what happened to her. She had to save her Britney from this evil force.

Just as she put the car into gear, she heard the back door open. Britney jumped in. "Mom, I'm coming. I want to ride with you." At first Janna was livid, but suppressed her emotions. Then there was a flood of relief. She had an excuse to postpone the inevitable. The unthinkable. They drove to Hanna's house in silence. Only a postponement. Janna was sure of that.

Chapter 40

The doctor was drenched in perspiration, and exhausted. He sat down in resignation on the edge of the examining table, next to Miss Shaw's slowly cooling body. His eyes roamed madly around the room, looking for something that might get him out of this fix. They stopped and focused on a hypodermic needle lying on the instrument tray.

Could he do it? Just suck some air into it and plunge it into his arm, waiting for the air bubbles to hit his heart and end it all? But he knew he was a coward at heart. The concept of death, so near, almost made him soil his pants.

His ravings were suddenly interrupted by the shaking of and sharp poundings on the entry door. He leaped to his feet, his former panic now back again in full force. Mary's muffled, angry voice came from the other side of the thick metal portal.

Brad's mind raced. The needle was still tantalizingly close. He picked it up and drew the plunger back. His reciprocal anger at the unexpected intrusion rose to the bile of a full rage as he thought about his last few years with his wife. How spoiled and lazy she had become. Yes, the lack of sex was mostly his fault, because the reality of laying with her couldn't come close to reaching the thrill of his sex with his patients. But she just sat around the house all day unless she was out spending voluminous amounts of money, allowing him to carry the awful burden of supplying the funds for her habit.

What happened next was a dream. He cracked the door open, and invited her in. Closing the door behind her, he muffled her mouth with his left hand and drove the sharp point into her bicep, expertly emptying the invisible contents into her. Her screams came out as mousey squeaks.

Mary's last vision was of Vanessa Shaw lying on the table, her eyes wide open in death.

Chapter 41

At first Billy could not believe he was freed from his confinement to the pipe. But with that freedom came a growing apprehension. What would Martha do to him once she found out he had been able to break the pipe? Visions of the glint of the carving knife made his heart pound in his chest and the sweat to form on his brow. He had to get out and away – to some place safe. The police? Billy's mom had taught him never to trust them. She had been arrested enough to instill that belief in him. So where?

Then Billy remembered the few times he had been in church: once or twice with his mother when the craziness had brought her to seek solace somewhere else than the bottle; and the times with auntie, when she could get him up to go. He thought he could find it. Someone there must be willing to help him.

As silently as he could, Billy laid the chain to one side, and got up. As near as he could tell, it was very early morning, as the light casting through the tiny window had an orange glow. With any luck, Martha and George would still be sound asleep. He had to be careful going up the cellar stairs, as it was still fairly dark, there were no railings, and his hands were cuffed. Shuffling a bit because of the stiffness in his knees and legs from such a long period of inactivity. Billy climbed the stairs one at a time, touching the edge of each upcoming tread with both hands to steady himself and find his way. At the top, he reached unsteadily for the doorknob. It wouldn't budge. They had locked him in! He should have expected that! Billy almost collapsed in frustration. Now he was dead. They'd discover the broken pipe and kill him.

With one last burst of resolve, Billy tried the knob again. To his amazement, after an initial resistance, it gave way and the door swung open. Thank God for these old fixtures, he said to himself with a rare smile. It was only moments later that he walked out the back door and into the blessed clean air. He filled his lungs with it as if it were the first breath he'd ever taken.

╫ ╫ ╫
Chapter 42

It was Wednesday evening, so Mr. Samuel Pritchard and Mrs. Amanda Murray-Pritchard were out to dinner. Sam had used his skills as an amateur calligrapher to prepare formal invitations for the two of them to go to Chardonnay's, their favorite French restaurant in the area. It was a whole hour's drive each way, but well worth it. The *Boeuf Bourguignon* alone was to die for, much less drive for.

Sam and Mandy had kept alive the tradition of a weekly "date night" during their marriage. They were the only of their married friends and acquaintances who did it regularly. They were proud of that fact — not smug — but proud. It was always a meaningful event for them, and they tried to stay away from any unnecessarily serious subjects and simply enjoy each other's company. That was not difficult for them. They truly liked one another, which they both felt was a necessary ingredient in any love relationship.

Sam opened the door for Mandy, and could not help but notice her slim figure tightly wrapped in her, and his, favorite little black dress, a figure accentuated by her tiny feet snug in black high heels. A string of small, natural pearls adorned her neck. She had that fresh, just bathed smell and look that he loved so much. Made him want to caress her softly, and ravish her, all at the same time. On her part, Sam looked so debonair in his tan silk sports coat and deep blue shirt with the collar open. Her thoughts about him could turn equally lascivious … quickly.

On the way to the restaurant, Mandy chattered easily about her day in classes, some of her classmates, her professors. To Sam, law school sounded like a series of days at the zoo: in the primate section, with the noisy, argumentative chimps; with the birds, the strutting peacocks and preening cockatoos; and also the large cats, the dangerous and agile leopards and tigers. He never tired of her stories. There was the guy who wore a three piece suit, complete with silk paisley tie and matching handkerchief, to every class, standing out boldly against the uniform denim shirts, jeans, and sandals that prevailed in the school. Not to omit the gaggle of feminists, always with bad breath, who nitpicked over every slight of gender, real or imagined. And her torts professor who was certifiably nuts: a wild, unpredictable man who illustrated his legal points with stories about the fictitious African tribe 'The Fugawe's', and who suffered a literal breakdown in class on almost a weekly basis. It was not mere coincidence that Mandy, naturally very intelligent but sweet and unpretentious, had made no real friends in the school.

Mandy had her 'Moot Court' argument that day, an annual

rite where the students are given a case — a set of facts with an imaginary outcome in a lower court — and they have to take sides and prepare appellate briefs seeking to sustain or overturn that decision. The exercise is capped by a final argument before a tribunal consisting of two upperclassmen and a law professor. The annals of law school history are rife with anecdotes of the cruelty of the event — the meanness of tone, the purposely embarrassing and confusing questions that pepper the participants — all in the name of toughening them up for the big game. But Mandy had come out of it voted "best speaker" of the contest, meaning she had delivered the most professional, convincing oral argument, not an award to be disdained. So she was a little full of herself this day. In Mandy's nice way.

Sam was dutifully impressed. "Baby cakes, that's fantastic. 'Best speaker!' I could have saved them some time and told them beforehand what a talker you were!"

"Thanks for sparing me the embarrassment, my adoring husband," Mandy sparred back.

"What fascinating things happened in the health world today?" Mandy knew that much of Sam's day was spent in the exhausting completion of mounds of paperwork, at all levels of government — the federal, state, county, and local — the demand for covering your ass documentation was never-ending. It was obviously the part of the job he liked least.

"A lot of the usual today. Had to check out a couple of overflowing septic tanks; some complaints that landlords weren't providing sufficient heat. Nothing exciting. Finally got that guy to comply with the condemnation order. Received a call from the wrecking company – they're slated to begin demolition next week. That's a relief."

"You mean Tom Smalley? He finally relented? That's great!" Mandy knew Smalley had been a thorn in her husband's side for almost a year now. He had litigated Sam's decision that one of his rotten tenements had to be torn down – despite the fact that it was overwhelmingly clear the building was beyond repair and presented an obvious danger to the public.

There was a pause in the conversation. Sam reluctantly brought it up. He knew it was foremost on their minds, so better to clear the air.

"I had that conversation with Dr. Henderson."

"Oh really?" Mandy replied.

"Yeah. I spoke to him right after we got off the phone."

"Did he have anything to say?"

"It was more what he didn't say. He denied knowing anything about the Sandoz family. It was just his hesitation. The change in his tone of voice while we discussed it. That's why I feel he was lying to me. I've felt it since the first time I met him. The guy's just a damn liar. And I don't think he's being

-153-

completely truthful about the possibility that DMT has polluted our water. Or what the ramifications of that could be."

Mandy cut in: "For me – and I've never spoken to the man – it's more the complexity of the network of corporations and trusts that he devised. No one does that unless they've got something to hide. I mean, he's supposed to be a college professor and researcher. Why'd he need this legal quagmire to attain his goals? I think the reason is obvious."

Sam responded. "Hide what? That he was engaged in a criminal enterprise? But what kind? How does it relate to his research on DMT? Those are the questions I'd like to have answered. Because I think it may help us solve the mystery of what in the hell has been going on here in Cary."

"I think you're right honey. Let's continue looking into this. But, again, I have this feeling. Call it woman's intuition if you will. We have to be very careful."

"We will sweetheart. Let's start by agreeing we won't discuss these matters with anyone but ourselves. Okay?"

"You got it babe."

They arrived at the restaurant, and had a great meal, being careful not to delve into, or even mention, the prior subject. They did so totally unaware that a hulk of a man was sitting in a car across the street from their home, watching for any sign of life within.

CHAPTER 43

Dr. Henderson was just settling down in his favorite TV chair. The frozen meal was out of the microwave and on the tray table beside him. A glass of red wine stood next to it. This was his quiet time, he thought. The wife was away visiting her elderly parents. No children, thank God. He had no time for a pack of little brats running around the place. Life was not so bad. Especially with the real estate, solely in his spouse's name, and hundreds of thousands of dollars sitting in bank accounts around the world, much of it in his beloved sister's name.

But it had been a difficult week. What with that snotty-nosed health guy poking around into everyone's business. Richard also hadn't liked the tone of Sandoz's voice when Richard told him about his conversation with Pritchard. Sandoz was not a man to be fooled with.

With a start Henderson knocked the wine to the floor, shattering the glass and spraying the red substance across the hardwood . He had suddenly sensed the presence of another man. Close by. Was it breathing he heard? Or a distinctive, foreign odor?

The man stepped around the corner of the doorway leading to the adjoining room. A very large man. Richard started to get up, but sat back down when the man said, "Stay seated, Henderson. I'm just here to have a little chat with you. If you try to get up, I'll just knock you back down."

"How did you get in here?" Richard asked in a shaky voice.

"Never mind that. Just know I can appear and disappear wherever you are, at any time of night and day." The man sat down in a chair about six feet from where Henderson was sitting. He was a towering presence. A malignant presence.

"I want you to tell me exactly what you told those two health inspectors. The first time they came to see you. And more recently when you spoke to the young one. Don't leave out a single detail."

"Sandoz sent you, didn't he?" the Doctor queried.

The man brought his huge fist down hard on the table next to him, making a sound like a thunderclap. Henderson jumped about three inches out of his chair.

"I'm asking the questions here," he bellowed. "Now tell me what I came here to find out."

Dr. Richard Henderson nervously relayed as best he could his conversations with Sampson and Pritchard. The man interrupted often, demanding more detail or cutting Henderson off when he started to ramble from the subject.

"So are you telling me you never ... and I mean never ...

mentioned to either of them that Mr. Sandoz was connected to any of the trusts or corporations?" the man asked.

His suspicions confirmed as to who had sent the man, Henderson said, "You can tell Mr. Sandoz ... I mean you can *assure* Mr. Sandoz ... that I never said anything about him. Never, as you say, mentioned anything about him. You have my word on that."

The man grunted, paused to think a moment, and asked: "Where do you keep the records of your bank accounts? Your financial records?"

"Why do you want to know that?" Henderson said, very concerned now.

The huge man suddenly stood up, surprisingly quick and agile for his size, and screamed: "I'll break every bone in your body, Henderson. Slowly. Tell me where the records are!"

"Calm down. Calm down!" Henderson pleaded. "I'll tell you everything you want to know. Just settle down."

The man sat back down, never taking his eye off of Henderson.

"Tell me then. Now!" he demanded.

"I will. But I just need to know I'll be safe after I tell you. Otherwise, there wouldn't be any purpose to me for telling you. Right?" Richard babbled.

"All you should care about is whether you're safe right

now. And believe me, you're not. Look. Sandoz just wants to know you've got them in a secure, safe place. They contain some information that might lead to him. So where are they?"

"My attorney has most of the records," Henderson lied. "There might be some around here. I'm just not sure. I can let you know exactly where they are in a few days."

The big man walked slowly over to the broken glass on the floor as if to pick it.

"Gotta be mighty careful of this. Wouldn't want anyone to get hurt."

He suddenly pirouetted around and slapped Richard as hard as he could across the face. The force of the blow whipped his head around and momentarily rendered him unconscious. In a few seconds he came to, and instinctively raised his hand in front of his face. Tears swelled in his eyes.

"Goddamn it! What'd you do that for?"

The man raised his other hand as if to strike.

Richard wailed: "Please stop! I'll show you. I'll show you," he repeated. "Just don't hit me again!"

The big man backed away a few feet, and with a graceful sweep of his arm, motioned Henderson to proceed in the direction of the records, wherever that might be. Richard got up, slowly and carefully, always keeping an eye on his adversary. He began walking toward a large painting overhanging the fireplace.

The man gave some leeway to let him get there. Richard lifted the painting and set it aside, exposing an expensive, very secure looking wall safe.

"Everything's in here," Henderson said nonchalantly, as he expertly twisted the dial. The tumblers fell into place with a click, and the Doctor pulled the handle and opened the safe while still carrying on some banter about how much the safe cost, how hard the installation was. His hand remained in the safe for a few seconds, as if he were leafing around for papers. Suddenly he turned, a Force nine mm pistol in his hand, a surreal grin on his face. "Now you bas . . ." His turn was met with a .38 Magnum slug directly between the eyes. Henderson blew backwards, slammed against the hearth, and crumpled to the floor, dead as a doornail.

"Nice try," the man said. "Forgot to tell you I know your kind."

He emptied the safe of its contents, stuffed them in a log carrying satchel next to the fireplace, and left the premises.

Chapter 44

The dreams were coming back. With a vengeance. There was hardly a night when Janna didn't awake in a cold sweat from one of them. All of the same genre: always the cold, sterile operating room; the floating; the light ahead; the dreadful darkness behind … constantly pulling her … pulling her backward toward the abyss.

She decided to take a drive. It was a beautiful Fall day. The air crisp and clean. Just the atmosphere to clear her head. She made sure her dad was home to watch Britney, then hopped in the car and took off. No particular place to go. In no particular direction.

The comfort of the autumn leaves, their variegated colors, reflecting the lowering sunlight, left her peaceful for the first time in days. Aimlessly she drove, only admiring what nature presented to her.

Janna awoke from her reverie with a start. Wasn't this Elaine's and Hanna's neighborhood? How did she end up here? Suddenly the tranquility that had enveloped her turned to a foreboding fear. Had she intended to go here? She drove past their house, turning her head so no one would spot her.

As she neared the intersection at the end of the street, she slowed her pace, and pulled to the side of the road. Something to her right had attracted her attention. It was a brief flash of pink, and of blond curls bouncing on the back of a neck. Of a small girl. Janna couldn't believe her eyes. There was Hanna, heading toward the corner. She watched as the young girl waited for traffic to clear, then crossed the street and entered a convenience store a half block from the intersection.

Janna was suddenly filled with rage. Why was Hanna allowed such freedom when Janna would never allow Britney out of her sight? Did Hanna think she was that special? That superior to Britney? Just because she had such a beautiful face, and that gleaming light hair with its natural curls. Is that what made her so smug? So condescending? Janna could barely contain her anger.

Janna waited in her car until she saw Hanna exit the store. Hanna paused at the intersection again to wait for traffic. Janna gunned her vehicle, and going down the wrong side of the street, pulled next to the little girl. Hanna jumped back, a little frightened.

Janna leaned out the window. "Hanna, darling. I can't believe it's you! What a coincidence. Are you going home?"

Now recognizing her friend's mom, Hanna came forward. "Hi Ms. Gleason. I didn't know it was you. Is Britney with you?"

"No honey. She's at home. I was just going to the store," pointing with her hand to the place Hanna had just left.

"Why don't I give you a lift home. Or better yet, why not come back with me and visit Britney for a while. She's been alone all day and would love to see you. Okay?"

"But my mommy's expecting me right back. I can't go anywhere."

"Aw, come on sweetheart. We'll call your mom as soon as we get to our house. It'll only take a few minutes. Britney would be really happy to see you."

"Well, alright," Hanna said. "But only for a little while. I really must get back soon."

Hanna got into the passenger seat and buckled her seat belt as she had been consistently taught to do. Three minutes into the drive, Janna turned to Hanna and said, "I'm sorry honey. I just remembered what I needed at the store. You don't mind if we stop briefly, do you? It's only a short distance away."

"But Ms. Gleason, I do need to get home."

Janna's bile rose into her throat. "You little asshole. I told you we'd be there soon. Now we're going to the store, and that's all there is to it!"

Hanna started to quietly whimper. Janna gave her no comfort. Janna took a left down a narrow dirt road just past a small groceria. Hanna's whimpering became a little more pronounced, as if she sensed something was very amiss.

Proceeding down the road about a mile, Janna pulled into a slight clearing, making her car difficult to see unless someone passed directly by. She sat for a moment, enjoying the child's light crying.

Janna started speaking softly. At first.

"You really think you're the cat's meow, don't you Hanna? Think you've got it all. Well I've got something to tell you. You don't!" Now Janna's voice was rising, taking on an angry tone.

"My Britney has it all over you. You may not think so. But I know so! How dare you mock her. How dare you!" Janna was spitting out the words, her face contorted with the increasing fury. Hanna looked away as if by doing so she could avoid the coming maelstrom.

"Don't you ignore me! Don't you look away. You're feeling guilty now, aren't you? Look at me!"

With that Janna grabbed a clump of the girl's curls and twisted her head around. Hanna let out a shrieking wail, her eyes wide with fear. Janna grabbed her around the neck and began shaking her, her thumbs digging deep into the center of the girl's throat. Hanna began struggling violently, her breath being choked out of her – clawing, kicking, anything to release the death grasp Janna had on her. But the five year old's struggles were nothing against the intensity of the adult's purpose.

Slowly Hanna's resistance subsided, in increments, Janna's pressing continuing unabated. Finally Hanna's head slumped to one side, her body limp. Only then did Janna begin to release her grip. She watched as the small body seemed to fold against the door.

Janna sat for a few minutes, her energy totally sapped. She was shaking all over. Then a growing exhilaration began to fill her. Triumphantly, she thought, now what will Elaine think! How she'll suffer, like I've been suffering. I've won! I've taken her darling Hanna from her. I won't have to put up with the ridicule, the condescension any more!

Then Janna's instinct of self-preservation began to kick in. I've got to get rid of the body! She noticed the blood lightly creeping through her shirtsleeves where Hanna's nails had bitten deep as she fought. I've got to change my clothing and destroy these. A plan began to develop.

When she had gotten her shaking under control, Janna exited the car, walked around to the back, and opened the trunk. She then went to the passenger door, opened it, and lifted Hanna's body out of the seat. She was heavier than she thought she would be. Dead weight, she thought happily. Unceremoniously she dumped the body into the trunk, Hanna's head bouncing sharply off the car jack lying on the floor.

Janna drove home slowly, not wanting to attract any attention to her car or where she had been. Arriving home and parking outside the little house, Janna went in, voicing a light 'Hello' to her father who was sitting in front of the television. She went upstairs. Luckily Britney was playing by herself in the back yard, and didn't notice her mom's arrival.

She changed all of her clothes, and rolled the old set into a ball and placed them in a plastic bag. Next she carefully washed her arms, and applied a mild anti-bacterial ointment. Pulling a large suitcase down from the upper shelf of her closet, she placed the bag of clothes inside, and quietly walked downstairs and out the door. The pastor never saw her leave.

Remembering she had passed an irrigation ditch on the way down the dirt road, and the privacy afforded by the clearing, she headed for it. It didn't take long to get there and place the small body in the suitcase. Janna worked methodically, as if she were performing any normal task, but without any feeling. It took a little effort to arrange the body to fit into the suitcase without allowing noticeable bulges in the center.

Pulling up to the ditch with the motor running, and looking carefully around her, Janna removed the suitcase from the trunk, and with some effort, dragged it to the edge. Positioning it so it would hit the center of the small body of water, she sat it on it's edge, and pushed it in. A momentary panic struck her when the suitcase floated briefly on the surface of the water. Within seconds, however, it settled, tipped to one side, and slowly slid into the murky void.

✟✟✟
Chapter 45

Pastor Dan and Bob Anders had scheduled an early morning meeting to discuss the Ernie Bates matter. Although it was Sunday, not even the first volunteers had arrived to prepare the church for the busy day. They were in the Pastor's office next to the vestibule, and had a clear view of the entrance way.

Bob was talking. He was a little rough around the edges, but he at least spoke his mind and there was no bullshit.

"Pastor, Ernie's really worryin' me. I've tried to reach him several times, and gotten no response. I left some messages with his wife, and I presume he got 'em, but still nothin'. I even stopped by the other day. Had this weird feelin' he was there, but no one answered the door. Has anyone said anything to him?"

"Not after the meeting, as far as I know. I think everyone is waiting for the next meeting when we'll discuss the matter. Guess I should give him a call."

"I'd really appreciate it if ya would. He's been a good friend. First one to approach me when I got outta the can. I'd hate to see anything happen to him."

Bob paused for a few seconds as his attention was diverted to the front sidewalk leading to the church. "What in God's name is that!?" he shouted.

Dan sat bolt upright. The two men turned their attention to a hunched figure limping toward the building. Its hair was wild and disheveled, the clothing blood soaked, torn and soiled. It appeared as more an apparition than human. Unrecognizable. The figure dropped to its knees at the door, then rolled over and lay down in the fetal position.

Dan and Bob instantly jumped to their feet and rushed to the door. Opening it carefully so as not to hit the body, they knelt in unison by it.

"Oh my God, it's Billy," Dan cried out. "Let's get him to the day care room. There's a cot there."

Bob leaned over, gently took the boy in his massive arms, and carried him to the bed. Billy's stink was overpowering, but Bob was not fazed. He asked Billy softly if he could get anything for him? Water? Food? When the child nodded at the word water, Dan ran out and filled a glass. Bob put the water to his lips, and Billy drank hungrily, sputtering occasionally as he took in too much.

Sensing Billy was too far gone to talk, to tell them what had happened, Dan initially suggested that they call the police. Bob countered with the idea that he take him home and care for him. His sister, who was a nurse, was in town and could assist.

"Why don't we make sure he's alright, get him cleaned up, and then decide what to do. I'd like to hear what happened. I'll tell you this, Pastor, if Martha and George had anything to do with this, there's gonna be some righteous discipline administered," Bob warned.

☨ ☨ ☨
Chapter 46

Doctor Wilson quietly exited the room, being sure that the push lock was engaged as he closed the door. He passed by the horrified countenance of Susan, giving her only a quick wave as he exited. He drove immediately to his bank, where he withdrew just under ten thousand dollars, the maximum amount to avoid federal reporting requirements. Pointing his vehicle toward the west, he high-tailed it to the remoteness of the Rockies, some five hundred miles distant.

Susan waited a respectful fifteen minutes after the doctor had left, then went to the door and knocked lightly. When heavier raps elicited no response, she tried the door. It was locked. She knew three people had entered the room, and only one had exited. Unless she had missed anyone? She didn't think so, but she wasn't one hundred per cent sure.

After a few more minutes, she walked outside and around to the side window looking into the examining room. Unfortunately the examining table was facing away from the window, and the back was elevated, preventing her from seeing what, if anything was on it. Moreover, gossamer white curtains created only a fuzzy image of what she could see.

She went back to her station. Unfortunately she was the

only one left in the office, the nurse having taken off two hours earlier. She had no idea what to do. Call the police? What if they found the room empty, both Vanessa and Mary somehow having found their way out? How embarrassing that would be!

Her thoughts were interrupted as a man walked through the front entrance door. She immediately recognized him as Vanessa Shaw's dad, coming to pick her up. He was a very large man.

"Hi Mr. Shaw. What are you doing here?"

"Well, I'm here to pick up Vanessa, of course."

Susan's sudden look of dread was not missed by the man.

"What's wrong? Is Vanessa okay? Did something go wrong with the exam?" he roared.

"I ... I don't know, Mr. Shaw," Susan managed to get out. "I thought ... maybe ... she had already gone home with you."

"What do you mean! Where is she?!"

Susan tried to explain as best she could what she had seen. As she did so, the horror of the situation became more evident.

"Show me where the examining room is. Now!" the father yelled.

He tried the doorknob. Nothing had changed. He tried the door with his shoulder., but it wouldn't budge. Mr. Shaw was not a man to be dissuaded easily, especially where his daughter's safety was involved. He gave the door five mighty hefts with his huge frame. Finally it dislodged from it's top hinges, affording them enough space to climb up and over into the room.

"What the ... !" Susan shouted. There was a large bulge on the table, as if pillows had been carelessly tossed on it, covered by a sheet. Mr. Shaw walked over, and with a quivering hand, reticent to discover what was beneath, pulled the sheet back from the head of the bed. There were Vanessa and Mary, lying side by side, their arms partially embracing each other in a death lock, rigor mortis already progressing through their bodies.

╫ ╫ ╫
Chapter 47

Pedro and Jose needed a break. The weather had been viciously hot for a week now. Not only that, the boss man had to go into town to get some spare parts for the tractor. So they were able to sneak away without being seen to some trees by a ditch.

They sat down in the shady spot and talked a little about going back to Mexico the following month. They had had enough. The rosy future set before them by Pablo never materialized. He took most of their life savings – a couple thousand dollars – to sneak them across the border and arrange for a job in the States.

Since then their lives had been a living hell. A typical story – they made just enough to pay the boss man for their room and board and a few luxuries, like tobacco and some beer. The promised bonuses were still just that – empty promises. And that was almost a year ago.

Pedro spotted it first. The heat and lack of rain had sucked most of the stale water out of the ditch. Barely visible above the surface of what little liquid remained was the corner of a suitcase. One metal latch glinted off the intense sunlight.

"Mi amigo. Look at that. What is it?" he asked.

"No se," his friend responded. "Is it a case?"

The two men used one of their extension pruners to reach across the ditch and hook the object under it's handle. They were surprised to find it so heavy that it kept slipping off the pole. Finally they were able to work it over to their side so they could grab it.

"Dios!. There is something very heavy inside," exclaimed Jose. Pedro had sudden visions of untold riches. Was it cash? Coin? If so, what shape would it be in? It smelled bad, but that could be because of the mud and rotting vegetation that coated it's sides.

The middle latch wouldn't budge. So Jose took out a large pocket knife and snapped it open with a quick upward thrust. They then slowly undid the side buckles.

The suitcase was only open a fraction of a inch when the two man jumped backward. The stench was like a blow to the face.

"Que Diablo!" Pedro screamed. There was clearly something dead – that had been dead quite a while – inside. They stood back about ten feet and carefully lifted the top of the case with the blade end of the same pole they had used to extract the suitcase. There, covered with slim and partially eaten by bugs and worms, was the body of a young girl, huddled into the fetal position.

✝✝✝
Chapter 48

Sandoz' hands were still shaking after he hung up the phone. He couldn't believe his ears. He had unwittingly unleashed the dogs from Hell.

He had been surprised to hear Mike's voice on the other line. He seldom called unless Sandoz had initiated a communication. The conversation had gone something like this:

"It's done." No hello. No how are you. His deep, emotionless tone.

"What d'ya mean, 'it's done?' What does that mean, Mike?"

"It's done, asshole. The job is done. Henderson's dead. And now I'm goin' after that little faggot health inspector."

Harold's pause on the line apparently was a little too long. Mike had hung up just before he screamed into the phone, "You fuckin' crazy bastard! I didn't tell you to kill him. You were just supposed to …." Then the disconnected call tone interrupted. Sandoz attempted twice to call the pay phone number back, but it wouldn't take his return call.

Now what was he to do? He had done a lot of terrible things in his life, but never murder. Or a double murder. He'd never had blood on his hands. His consternation was more the fear of being caught, of life in a horrible, filthy prison or even worse, than it was the concept of taking another life.

Sandoz paced the room, trying to settle down, to think. He had to do something. Another killing would just increase the chance that Mike would be apprehended, and Sandoz entertained no doubts if that happened, Mike would rat on him in a heartbeat to get a more favorable deal.

It suddenly came to him. He had to try to warn Pritchard. If he could get to him, without disclosing his identity, possibly he could thwart Mike's attempt on his life. But remaining *incognito* was paramount. Harold ran to his upstairs closet and grabbed a baseball cap and some sunglasses. He then quickly looked up Pritchard in the phone book. Thank God he was listed. Hurriedly writing down the address and phone number, Sandoz hopped in his car and went to the nearest pay phone at the gas station about a half mile from his house. Repeatedly he called the number, only to get the recording of a pleasant male voice:

"Hello. This is the home of Sam and Mandy. We're sorry we missed your call, but leave your name and number and we'll get back to you as soon as we can."

Afraid to leave a permanent record of his voice on the machine, Sandoz got back in his car and headed to the Pritchard's home.

Chapter 49

Sam and Mandy had thoroughly enjoyed their night out. Maybe a tad too much Savignon Blanc, but Sam was fine to drive home. Despite the bucket seats in their Ford Mustang, they found a way to snuggle against each other. They giggled, talked a little dirty, and listened to their favorite lite jazz station during the entire ride.

Sam pulled carefully into their driveway. It was narrow, what with the neighbor's hedge which directly abutted. He was oblivious to the dark car and occupant parked one house down and across the street.

Mike watched as the car pulled up and the man and woman emerged and went into the house. This was not good. He was hoping to find Pritchard by himself. But if he had to kill both of them, so be it. He fingered the smooth silencer on his .38.

Sam and Mandy decided to have one night cap and watch a re-run of Sex in the City. Sam selected a brawny port from among their small collection of aperitifs. They settled down in front of the tube on the large, overstuffed couch in their living room which faced the street.

Exiting his car and soundlessly closing the door, Mike

walked toward the home. He wanted to take them by surprise to avoid any unnecessary commotion. His lock pick set was stowed in a small bag hooked to his belt. Making his way to the rear of the house, he kept low so as not to be observable from inside.

Sandoz proceeded slowly down the street, trying to make out the numbers in the dark. 510, 508 . . . that white gambrel with the green shutters must be it. He pulled to the curb one house down, turned off the ignition and lights, and sat for a few moments to collect his thoughts. Just a knock on the door, a quick and sincere warning, and then out of there. He would have done everything he could do without jeopardizing his identity. It was up to Pritchard from that point on.

The couple sleepily watched their re-run. Both were quite tired from the evening, and probably should have hit the sack as soon as they got home.

Mandy sat bolt upright. "What was that?"

"Whaaat?" Sam responded, suppressing a yawn.

"No honey. Seriously. I heard something." The urgency in her voice instantly dispelled Sam's grogginess and brought him to a heightened state of alertness.

Sam, ever the one to hog the remote, muted the sound on the T.V. They both sat for a few seconds without taking a breath. There it was. A barely perceptible scratching sound at the back door. The door then jiggled a little. Instinctively, Sam reached under the couch, and in one motion, slipped out a small case.

He opened it using his thumb to deftly turn and align the combination numbers, and pulled out a Kimber Rimfire Target Pistol, one of the finest and most accurate made.

The ringing of the front doorbell made both of them jump out of their skins. Mandy let out a gasp. Sam, now not knowing whether to cover the front or the back, opted for the more visible front door. Grabbing Mandy's hand and the phone, Sam led her behind the large, wing-backed chair in the room, and told her to dial 911.

Slowly approaching the front door, Sam was able to see a figure in a baseball cap and sunglasses, despite the time of night, standing on the porch. Sam yelled through the glass: "I don't know who you are, but I've got a gun. Leave this property at once."

The man yelled back. "Mr. Pritchard. You are in grave danger. Someone is after you. That's all I can say right now."

Mandy screamed: "Honey. Watch it! Behind you!"

Sam turned suddenly toward the sound of her voice. At that moment a bullet grazed his left shoulder and shattered a section of the front door glass. Sam dove to his side, sliding across the polished, hard wood floor, and fired three shots in less than a second. All found their target, making a neat triumvirate around Mike's heart. He was dead before the back of his head rebounded off the tiled floor in the entryway from the kitchen. Sam jumped up, ran to the body, and kicked away the silenced gun which still clung perilously to the man's fingers. Leaning down, he futilely searched for a pulse on the man's beefy neck.

Mandy yelled again. "Sam! The man out front!"

Getting up, Sam shouted to Mandy if she was all right as he ran toward the front, his pistol up and ready for more action. Mandy nodded yes, and Sam carefully approached the door, staying low. A round hole, about three inches in diameter, had been blown out of the stained glass panel adorning the center of the door. Sam peered through it, pointing his gun toward it at the same time. The figure, now easily identifiable as a man, lay on his back on the porch, his hat and sunglasses having been blown off with the impact. A neat hole in the center of his forehead was oozing a pinkish, yellowish fluid, while dark, maroon blood formed a puddle behind his head. Mr. Sandoz had met an unfortunate end.

✞✞✞
Epilogue

Janna was charged with the first degree murder of Hanna. She was caught easily. While inspecting the suitcase, the cops found, tucked deeply into one of the small side pockets, an old plane itinerary from one of the times Janna had flown off to college. It didn't take long for the DNA found in her car to be matched up. Found guilty by a jury of her peers, despite her lawyer's energetic defense of not guilty by reason of insanity, she was sentenced to life imprisonment without a chance of parole. Her father obtained custody of Britney, and did his best to raise her in a God-fearing environment.

The police soon became involved in Billy's case. His injuries were too severe – especially the festering fracture in his elbow – to keep him away from the hospital. Both Martha and George were charged with first degree child endangerment. Martha got four to six years in state prison; George two and a half in the county jail. Billy stayed with Bob Anders and his sister, and finally found a safe haven with two people who grew to care for him deeply.

Brad was apprehended two states away, trying to make a break for it. Charged with both murders, he received a double life sentence.

Sam was absolved of any guilt in the two shooting deaths, there being ample evidence that the one he caused was in self-defense. He and Mandy moved far away. Sam landed a job with the federal government in Washington D.C at the Department of Human Services. But not until he had single-handedly orchestrated the shut down of the entire water system in the Town of Carey, and set up a massive clean-up project that took years to complete. Mandy transferred to Georgetown Law School and specialized in environmental law. They eventually had two kids – twin girls, Jessica and Julia – that they doted on.

Both federal and state investigations over the span of five years failed to establish any connection between the Superior Chemical spill and the behavior of the citizens of Carey, California.

╫ ╫ ╫
Postscript

This story is not that far-fetched. It is grounded in the real life events of Tracy, California, where a series of inexplicable events confounded law enforcement, and everyone else for that matter. For a brief glimpse of what went on there, go to: http://www.huffingtonpost.com/huff-wires/20090425/missing-girl-police/

The horror seems to still be visiting the Town: see http://www.tracypress.com/view/full_story/5144362/article-Teacher-gets-probation-on-molestation-charges

DMT is a fascinating, and disturbing, chemical. It has only been recently studied in depth (the past twenty years), and still remains a mystery to the researchers who have attempted to unlock its secrets. For further study, see:

1) DMT: The Spirit Molecule: A Doctor's Revolutionary Research into the Biology of Near-Death and Mystical Experiences, by Rick Strassman. http://www.rickstrassman.com/

2) http://en.wikipedia.org/wiki/Dimethyltryptamine
3) http://www.erowid.org/chemicals/dmt/dmt.shtml;
4) http://en.wikipedia.org/wiki/rick *strassman.*

Could the leakage of some chemical been the source of

the insanity that gripped Tracy? Could it have been DMT, or something similar to it? Or is it conceivable ... just conceivable ... that there is in reality an evil spirit, call it what you may, that lurks behind the gossamer fabric that separates the actual from the imagined and works its horror on us?

About the Author

Rusty Hodgdon is a graduate of Yale University where he majored in English Literature and Creative Writing. After graduating with a Juris Doctor degree from the Boston University School of Law, he practiced law for over twenty years in the Boston area, first as a Public Defender, then with his own firm. He left the practice of law and moved to Key West Florida to pursue his passion to write creative fiction. Rusty is also the winner of the 2012 Key West Mystery Fest Short Story Contest. All comments are welcome. Write to him at
RUSTY.THE.WRITER@GMAIL.COM

Made in the USA
Columbia, SC
17 October 2024

44556260R00114